D1732805

My testimony

Last year in December 2014, I was at my lowest.

Chasing a no good man, making myself sick and finding every

reason to blame myself. In between time, I wrote short

stories. I would write them as diary entries but they just so

happen to turn into my first book. In July I sent my manuscript

to JWP, just wishful thinking. Weeks passed and then I

received an email asking for the full manuscript :) overly

excited, I sent it right to her. A few days later I was signing my

contract. I still felt empty though, I was still looking for those

congratulations from that one man when the real man

congratulated me when he gave me my first breath. You can

worship man and fail but as long as you worship God, you'll

win. I finally caught on, and started reading my word and

learning the stories. I may slip up every now and then but all in

all, I've come a long way. At this point in my life, I'm just trying to find my true happiness and after so many prayers for the

perfect mate, I believe I'm being blessed in an unconventional

way. If I made it through 2014, everyone can make it through

2015.

Now I see how blessed I am :)

Dedications:

I dedicate this book to five people I can run to about any and

everything. You guys motivate me so much.

Thank you for EVERYTHING!

D.Willis

P.Hollifield

S.Bookman

J.King

K.Dunn

Acknowledgments:

To My readers/fans,

Thank you for the constant support and motivation. I really read the things you guys say and I take them into consideration. I hope you enjoy part two, ITS ABOUT TO GO DOWN!!!!!!

To My family & friends

Yall are my rock! I love you all so much! Thank you so much for believing in all my dreams no matter how crazy they are, you guys are always ready for the ride. Momma, I love you! Thank you for making me read and write at a young age, thank you for all the journals that I lost but found years later. Thank you for being YOU and having ME! I LOVE YOU MS.BARNER. Daddy I love you so much, you are my strength, you never gave up on your little black one no matter what I did. My light bright angel, Ba, I love you so much and miss you more than words can describe. I promised you that I'd make something of myself, even though my promise came late; I came through with great success. Ke Shai, my big little sister, thank you for never ever ever giving up on me. You're literally always down for the ride, no matter what my newest dream may be. I love you stuster. BFF, thank you for listening and supporting me in everything I think of, you are a best friend indeed. Nikki & Syd, I love yall with all my heart, I pray that im setting the bar high for you guys, shoot for the stars and believe me, and dreams do come true.

Momma Nae, you were around when I first started writing this as a short story for you guys to read around the office and look what we got now! You have supported me from day one and I appreciate all of it! TyBALDY, THANK YOU so much for all the support you've shown since we met. You are seriously one of my biggest supporters and everytime I want to give up, I think about the talk we had in my Everest days. You gave me so much life just from taking a chance and believing in me! I will always love you for that ☺ Lastly, my nephews, Khilen,Kase &KChaz, this is for you! I love you kays

☺

Thank you to all of you, EVERY SINGLE LAST ONE OF YOU.

Prologue

Xavier

8 months ago...

"Xavier, I don't know what to do. I seriously can't deal with his shit no more. Bitches sending me blind texts and calling my phone at all hours of the night, all because they want me to know that they messing with Stanley. I didn't sign up for this dumb shit at all," Lala said as she flopped down on my couch.

I just sat and listened to her, 'cause I didn't know exactly what to say. See, as a man, I was taught not to put my nose in another man's business. But that doesn't mean I'm heartless. I felt for the girl, no lie. Expletives and anger aside, she was obviously hurting. But Stanley and I been niggas since birth. He's my best friend. Not wanting to betray him, but wanting to console her, I reached over and rubbed her leg.

When Lala and her family first moved on the block, I had a little crush on her. I would catch her every time she decided to come outside, and would always try to start a conversation with her. At first, she was mean, but she ended up being cool as shit. She had a boyfriend when she first moved here; that punk ass nigga Tony. That nigga was a mark, and I could tell from the first day I saw him. I never disrespected their relationship. Yeah, I might've flirted a little here and there, but Lala would always keep things platonic. It was attraction at first sight for me when I saw her, so everything else fell into place once we began developing a friendship.

She looked up at me when I touched her thigh. I quickly moved my hand, thinking that I had crossed the line. Clearly, I was wrong, because she grabbed my hand and held it. I looked into her dark brown, very close to black, eyes, and I swear they said everything her mouth wouldn't. I wanted to pull away from her, but my body wouldn't let me. Lala. Sweet Lala. Touching me. My dick rose, letting her know how good this felt, how badly I wanted her. Thankfully, as I was sitting, she couldn't see.

"Lala, I...I think maybe you need to just talk to him one more time and tell him how you feel. Maybe he'll listen." I desperately tried to change from an embrace to a conversation.

She sighed. "Xavier, you know there's no talking to him. Once he feels like he's right, he doesn't have to say shit else. He won't even open the floor up to anyone else. It's always his way. You know what? I'm done. Just done!" Lala said as she stood up, and I assumed that she was leaving.

"Where are you going?" I asked, still sitting because I didn't want my erection to scare her.

"Imma go smoke or something. I need to clear my head," Lala replied.

I laughed. "Lala, I'm the weed man. Sit down."

She took her seat on the couch from where she'd just gotten up. I walked over to the table to get my box so I could roll her up a doobie.

"X, I don't like papers," Lala whined.

"Well, blunts are bad for you, so oh well."

She laughed at my response because it was the same every time she brought up a blunt. I sat down next to her again, this time concentrating on the doobie I was rolling up. She leaned back and exhaled. I looked over and watched her breasts rise and fall as she breathed in and out. My dick was throbbing at this point, and I knew that once I hit the weed, it would only get worse. Once I was done rolling up, I handed her the lighter and doob.

"Enjoy, Miss Lady," I said as I got up and walked out of the room. "I'm going to the bathroom. I'll be right back," I said as I left out the door.

Lala

Xavier has always been fine to me. His eyes were a delicious swirl of hazel and blue, and they always sucked me in, from the first time I saw him on the block. He always had a fresh cut, which was another thing that kept my attention. He was nice to all the kids on the street, and everybody respected him. I probably should have talked to him when I first moved, but my grandpa told me not to talk to anyone on the street, so I took heed to his advice and just kept my boyfriend that lived on the east side. If I had to choose anyone on the street to talk to, it definitely woulda been Xavier, but Stanley was more persistent when he started coming around. It's like Stanley saw me and knew he didn't really want me but kept me so nobody else could have me.

When Xavier walked out of the room, I flicked the lighter on the doob and took a deep hit. I tried to make the smoke stay in my lungs as long as possible. I wanted that good high, not no bullshit. I didn't even hear X when he walked back in the room. I just opened my eyes, and he was standing in front of me smiling.

"What you smilin' at?" I asked while trying to hide my own smile.

"Nothing, just watching you enjoy that," he said, nodding at the doobie in my hand.

I smiled and hit the doobie again, and this time I blew O's when I exhaled. The look on Xavier's face was priceless.

"Ha ha ha. What's wrong?" I asked as I coughed off the extra smoke in my throat.

Xavier walked over to me and sat on the other side of the couch, facing me.

"Pass it, stingy," he joked.

I passed him the doob, and he hit it. He closed his eyes. And as he enjoyed the dro, I couldn't help but stare at his beauty.

His eyes were the perfect shape for the perfect color that his eyes were, his high cheekbones gave his face a foreign type of look, and his hair was its own kind of beautiful. I imagined myself rubbing his head. His waves were as deep as real waves in the ocean. I could see myself tracing his lips with my tongue. He opened his eyes and caught me staring at him. I lowered my head in embarrassment. Neither one of us said anything. He passed the doob back to me, and I stood up to take it from him. I walked over to the couch he sat on and sat next to him.

"Wanna give me a charge?" I asked him.

I could tell he was caught off guard by my question, so I put the doob back in his hand and sat with my knees in the couch, facing him. He looked reluctant at first, but then he hit the doob. I puckered my lips, and he blew the smoke into my mouth. At this point, it was up to either of us to make the first move. I could feel the heat building up between us, so I made the first move. I grabbed his face and slipped my tongue in his mouth, not knowing if he'd accept it or deny me.

He greedily took my tongue into his mouth and sucked on it. I lifted myself off my knees, and I straddled him as he kissed me. I felt his hands roaming my body, which turned me on. His tight grip on my waist let me know that he felt the same thing I felt. I rotated in his lap as we got lost in each other's kisses. Taking my mouth away from his, I went on to trace his neck with my tongue. As I licked his neck, he found my spot—the spot right above my collarbone—and he went to work on it. I began humping him, childish I know, but shit, I could feel his dick growing in his basketball shorts. I knew what I wanted.

"Take this off," he said in a deep, sexy ass voice, referring to my T-shirt.

I sat up and lifted my arms, and he did the rest. His eyes lit up when he noticed I was braless. I don't know why he was surprised; I rarely wore bras anyway. He admired my breasts, the one thing I had a complex about. He noticed the scars that the surgeries of my past left, and he licked them. He took his time to lick every scar on my breast. Something no other man had done. He was accepting me.

The way he sucked on my nipple, I thought my nipple ring was going to end up down his throat. I moaned in ecstasy. The more he sucked, the wetter my pussy got.

"Fuck me," I finally said through clenched teeth, and it seemed like he was waiting for those exact words.

In a single, swift, almost cat-like motion, he ended up on top of me, and his basketball shorts were at his ankles. I laughed because he moved fast as hell. He untied the tie on my Hollister sweats and slowly rolled them down my legs and onto the floor. His eyes roamed my body, and I felt insecure and tried to cover myself with my hands. But he removed them.

"Move," he said as he continued to stare at me.

Xavier kissed my neck, down to my breasts, and he traced my stomach with his tongue before he came to a stop at my choc spot.

"She's so perfect," he whispered.

Before I could reply, his index and middle finger were inside of me, slowly hitting the walls of my pussy. I squirmed a little bit, but he held me in place.

"Stop moving," he instructed.

I did as I was told and laid there as still as possible. I closed my eyes to enjoy the treatment I was getting; I felt something warm. I opened my eyes and saw that his mouth was closing in on my pussy. I almost lost my mind as he ate me. His tongue went into places that no other man, not even Stanley, had ever touched. I lost my breath as he ate me. I tried to push his head away, but he only grabbed my tighter by the waist. He fucked me with his tongue until he had my cum dripping down his face.

When he came up for air, I attacked his mouth. I kissed him and sucked on his tongue. He slipped his fingers back inside of me as we kissed. I began humping his fingers and felt him smile against my lips.

"Ughhhhh. Fuck me" he grunted.

"Sit up," I told him.

When he sat up, I lifted myself right over him. His dick was standing straight up, and I couldn't wait to sit on it.

"Wait La, we need a rubber," he stopped me before I could take my seat.

"Do you have one?" I asked.

He looked around, thinking to himself and answered, "Nah, I don't think so."

"Just pull out," I said.

He looked at me weird, "You on birth control?" He asked.

"Nope, that shit makes me sick," I replied.

Everything went silent for a minute, and then out of nowhere, he pulled me down on his hard dick. I lost every bit of breath in my body.

He lifted me up and down on his dick until I caught on to his rhythm. His dick was so fat and long that it took a minute for me to be able to sit down on it completely, but, once I did, shit got real. I sat on his dick and moved back and forth, up and down. His head fell back against the couch, and he squeezed my ass hard as fuck.

"Ouch!" I yelled, but he didn't stop.

I grinded harder, and he went deeper. I tried to kiss him, but he moved his head and found my collarbone again. I stood up in a squat position and started bouncing on him. He liked it I could tell.

"Ahhhhhh, Lalaaaaaaa," he groaned in my ear.

I swear that made my pussy drip more. He found my nipple with his mouth again and began sucking on my nipple ring.

"Gimme that pussy, baby. Cum all over this dick." He egged me on as I rode him.

I reached behind me and played with his balls while I rode him. I felt his body tense up, and then he started lifting me and slamming me on his dick.

"Yessssssssssssss," I said as my breasts bounced in his face.

"You gone cum for me?" he asked.

I closed my eyes and put my hands on his chest to give myself leverage to move.

"Cum for me, La," he said as he grabbed my face and looked me in my eyes.

I think it was his eyes that released my orgasm.

"Oaaahhhhhhhhhhhhhhhh. I'm cumming, baby!" I said out of breath.

"Yesssssssssssss, that's it, baby. Lemme feel it."

I came so hard on top of X. I guess me cumming made him nut too because I felt his load shoot inside of me.

"Aaaahhhhhhhhh!!!!" He grunted as he held me still on top of him.

"Fuck! I'm sorry, Lala. I know I was supposed to pull out, but it felt too good. You felt too good, man," X explained as I sat on top of him catching my breath.

I was in so deep in "Lala land" that I didn't even realize he had actually cum in me.

"It's fine, I won't get pregnant," I responded as a matter of fact.

I didn't know if I was experiencing infertility, but I hadn't been pregnant since I was nineteen.

"How you know you won't get pregnant?" X asked.

"I just know. You good," I assured him as I kissed his forehead.

There was a minute of awkward silence, as neither one of us knew what to say. We knew what we'd done was wrong, but it was too late to go back. We sat in that position for what seemed like hours. Every time he got hard, I fucked him until he was soft again. This carried on until it was dark outside, and that's when I made my way back across the street. My walk of shame wasn't very shameful because nobody was outside, thankfully.

JESSICA WATKINS PRESENTS

LOVE, LIES, KARMA 2

by KIERA THOMAS

Xavier

"Laalaa. Ooohh, Lala," I moaned as I grabbed the back of her head and forced my dick farther down her throat.

She always gave me the best head, taking her time with the dick like it was a long Popsicle that she didn't want to waste. She licked the tip and down the sides, and she stroked 'em. Her mouth touching my balls always drove me insane.

"Ahhhhhh! I'm 'bout to nut," I said as I started pumping my dick in her mouth faster and harder.

I wanted her to gag, but she wouldn't. Or couldn't. Maybe her head game was just so good that nothing could make her gag. She grabbed my balls and sucked my dick as hard as she could, trying to get that nut out. Next thing I knew, I was exploding in the back of her throat.

I woke up sweaty and panting. That dream seemed so real. It felt even realer. I rolled over in the bed and regretted it as soon as I felt my morning wood.

Dick harder than Chinese arithmetic, I thought to myself with a chuckle.

I grabbed my phone off the nightstand. I had a few notifications: missed calls from the fiends, a few texts from a few chicks, nothing major. I scrolled down to Lala's name but

1

decided not to text or call her. I didn't know if Stanley was around or not. I sat up and threw my legs over the side of the bed and slid my feet into my Nike slides. Extending my arms above my head as I stood, I got a good stretch. I felt well rested. I guess that turtle juice put a nigga out. It was either that or the dro.

As I walked into the bathroom to take a piss, I heard my phone sound off. I flushed the toilet and washed my hands before walking out of the bathroom. When I reached my phone, it was going off again. I looked at the screen, and Lala's name illuminated across the screen. I flopped down on the bed and unlocked my phone and went to my inbox. When I scrolled down to Lala's name, a picture popped up once I opened the message. Her hazel-blue eyes were identical to mine. I blinked twice, just to make sure my eyes weren't deceiving me. When I opened my eyes after the last blink, the photo was still there, and I was still looking at a reflection of myself.

Lala

When I sent the picture to Xavier, I didn't know what his reply would be. This little thing of ours had gone on for a few months now. It seemed like every time Stanley was out of town, X was there to comfort me. We knew we were wrong, but it just felt too right. I love Stanley, but am I in love with him? Nah, I'm in love with Xavier, but I knew we would never be able to be together, considering my history with Stanley. I tossed my phone to the side of the hospital bed I was lying in. My nerves always get the best of me when I send important messages like that. Kamille was waking up anyway, so my baby doll needed all my attention.

I reached over to pick Kamille up out of the hospital crib they had her in. *My beautiful baby*, I thought to myself. She squirmed and began whining.

"Are you hungry, pretty?" I asked as I removed my breast from my bra.

I propped Kamille up on a pillow on my lap and tried to give her my nipple. She hasn't latched on yet, but I'm hoping today is the big day because it's so frustrating. I watched as she moved her head around under my nipple as if she was looking for it. Once she found it, she nibbled and completely latched on. As painful as it was, it felt good because, like I said, the shit was frustrating.

Stanley walked back in right on time to see Kamille being fed.

"Awww shit. She latched on, bae?" I nodded my head at him and smiled. He could tell I was excited. "Hey, my mom said when you get discharged to please stop by to see her first." He laughed as he spoke.

"You know yo' momma crazy," I replied with a chuckle.

"Yea, she something else," he said as he sat at the foot of the bed.

He stared at me while I held Kamille in my arms, and from his gaze, I could tell that something was on his mind.

"What's the matter, Stan?" I asked him.

He sat for a few seconds before he answered me, "It nothing really….well, I just wanna know if I should be worried about those paternity results."

He looked so sad as he spoke. I didn't know what to say to him at that moment. I mean, anyone in their right mind would be worried considering there are two...ok three, possible fathers. The only thing is that nobody knows about potential father number three, except for him and me.

"I mean, I was honest with you. I had slept with Tony around the same time. There's a chance she isn't yours, but there's a chance she is," I finally spoke up.

Stanley looked at me as if my last words hit him as hard as they did the first time I spoke them.

"I know it's a fucked up situation, but believe me, I didn't plan this, Stan. I would never make things complicated on purpose," I assured him.

"I know, La. I just wish shit was normal. It's just that; shit between us is always dysfunctional. It's like we're forcing something that's not meant to be."

My heart sank when he said that.

"What are you saying, Stanley?" I asked with tears in my eyes.

He sat quietly. He closed his eyes and opened them again and looked at me.

"I'm saying maybe we need a break for a minute."

He couldn't even look at me after he said it.

A part of me wanted to argue with him, but I knew it was probably for the best. I mean, I love Stanley, but Xavier has my heart, period. The hardest thing was hiding those feelings from Stanley and everyone else that knew us. I wasn't sure how things would play out, but I did know that if Stanley found out about Xavier and I, WW3 would pop off. I looked down at my beautiful engagement ring and thought about the night Stanley proposed and how I didn't want to say yes, but did it for my family. Truth is, I felt like Kamille not being Stanley's child would make it easier for me to walk away, but of course, nothing in life is that easy. I played with the ring on my finger, and when I looked up, Stanley was staring at me as if he'd be reading my mind the whole time.

I slid the ring off my finger and held it in my hand for a few seconds, wracking my brain to make sure I was making the best decision. Letting out a deep sigh, I finally had the nerve to hand the ring to Stanley as he sat at the foot of the hospital bed.

"I'm so sorry, Stan," I said as I handed him the ring.

He looked down at the ring sitting in the palm of his hand.

"Honesty is better than anything, La. I can't be mad at you for being honest with yourself and me." He spoke in a low tone, a very sincere one. "You've been through a lot lately. I am partially to blame for all of it, so I can't be upset. I love you, La, and I always will," he said as he stood to leave. "Let me know if you want me to come get you guys tomorrow; you can stay at the apartment. I'll go to mom's house until I find somewhere else to stay."

He bent down to kiss my forehead as he always did before leaving my side.

"Okay," is the only thing I could manage to say.

As relieving as it all was, guilt began to eat at me almost immediately.

Stanley

When I told Lala that we needed a break, I really expected her to go off and be mad, but she was the exact opposite, which let me know she was tired of my shit. I didn't expect her to give me back the engagement ring though. I don't know why I thought we could stay engaged as we worked out this whole paternity thing. Speaking of which, that shit had my head gone, so when I left the hospital, I called X to see what he was doing. I needed some turtle juice and shit, probably some weed too, even though I hardly ever smoke.

"What's happenin'?" X spoke into the phone after about three rings.

"Shit, nigga. Wassup with the juice? Who got it?" I asked.

"Uh, I don't know. I'm low right now, but Baby Rag probably got it. Lemme hit him."

"Aight, I'm on my way, so just tell cuh to pull up if he got it," I said before I hung up the phone.

I pushed the start button and started my car. "4 in the Morning" by Nipsey blasted out of the speakers. I nodded my head to the beat of the song; Nips was spitting some real shit. This song brought back too many memories. *Karisha.* "4 in the

Morning" was our anthem, back when she knew her role and played it well. I didn't always have problems out of Karisha; it wasn't until recently that she tried to take Lala's spot. Every bitch I fucked with knew about Lala and knew that there was no coming in between us. Karisha knew that, but she found herself in love with me, something I fed into because of the perks that came along with being with her. She paid for everything, anything she thought would make me love her, but I couldn't love her. I had love for her, but I would never be in love with a bitch like her.

I decided to make a pit stop at Long Beach Memorial where Karisha stayed. When I parked, I called her cell to make sure she was alone. The phone rang a few times before she picked up.

"Hello?" she answered.

"What up, man? Who at the hospital with you?" I got straight to the point.

"Nobody. I'm here alone," she replied.

I could kind of hear the excitement in her voice.

"Alright, here I come."

I hung up without saying goodbye. I got out of the car and made my way up to the part of the hospital she was at. She was no longer in ICU. I heard they moved her a day after she got there. Walking to the elevators, I turned my volume down on my phone, no interruptions.

Karisha

Stanley walked in looking like the man of the year. You couldn't tell these past few days affected him how they did me. His haircut was fresh, waves dipping, and line- up looking like it was done with a razor. He wore a white T-shirt, something he rarely does. He had on Hollister sweats and a fresh pair of 12's. The closer he got to the bed, the faster my heart started beating.

"Wassup?" he spoke, and my heart melted.

"Hi," I tried to fix my hair. "I know I'm looking rough, but give me a few days, and I'll be back to normal."

I tried to smile, but my face was so swollen that I doubted if he could tell I attempted to smile. He chuckled as he sat down in the chair closest to the bed, "You good, man. You look good for what you been through, cuh."

He was right.

"Thank you, Stan."

I tried to smile again, but this time I winched in pain because of the stitches in my lip.

"Stop tryna smile, fool," he laughed me. I tried to laugh with him, but the pain and soreness were just too much. "So, how you feeling?" He asked.

I looked at him like he was dumb. I wanted to get smart and ask the nigga, "How I look?" but instead, I cleared my throat and said, "I'm good, I guess."

I was debating whether I should tell him what I'd found out from the nurses a few hours ago. I decided against it; it wasn't the right time. I tried to adjust myself in the uncomfortable ass bed.

"How are you?" I asked.

He didn't answer right away; he just looked down at this hands that sat in his lap. Then the handcuffs on my wrist must've caught his attention.

"Have the police been here?" he asked.

"No, not yet. I think they're waiting on me to heal up so they can just take me in. She pressin' charges, huh?" I asked him.

I didn't want to think about being in jail in my condition, and something in me hoped he said, "Nah," but my heart knew it was the opposite.

"Yea, she ain't letting this shit go, man. I ain't talked to her about it, but she knows that you're alive and in the hospital. It's only a matter of time before the police contact her, and she'll fasho press charges," he replied.

He couldn't even look me in my face.

12

"You can't talk to her, Stanley? Buy the bitch a push gift or something! I *ain't* trying to go to jail." I spoke with attitude in my voice this time.

Horrified by the thoughts of my future, I was on the verge of going off on him.

"Karisha, you snuck into our baby shower and tried to kill her. You deserved everything you got, cuh. I can't do shit but let that girl do what she do."

His reply hit me hard. It hit me where it hurt the most. It was the truth, though. I wasn't supposed to be there, but of course, I let my emotions get the best of me and I showed up.

"I'm really not trying to go to jail, Stanley. I can't do it." I began to cry.

Shit was getting too real.

"You don't have a choice, cuh," he said with no feelings or emotions in his voice.

"I do, though," I said and looked at him so he could catch my drift.

"What the fuck you mean that you do? What the fuck you gone do, Karisha? Snitch?"

He looked at me like I lost my mind. I probably did, considering I just threatened one of the biggest, well-known Crips I knew.

"Nothing. I don't mean nothing," I said.

I tried to sit up in the bed.

"So what happens now, Stan? I just go to jail, and you and that bitch live happily ever after?" I spat at him.

My true feelings and anger began to slip out. He looked stunned when I said that to him.

"We aren't together anymore," he said as he hung his head. Those were the words I been hoping to hear for so long. "And if you get locked up, I'll look out for you since it's basically my fault."

I just looked at him. His eyes finally met mine.

"I love you, Stan."

I always said it, but he never would say it back to me.

"I love you, too." My heart melted, and I felt like shit was finally going my way. "I gotta go, cuh. I'll hit you up later to check on you. Keep this visit between us, Karisha."

He bent down to kiss my forehead as he stood to leave. I grabbed his neck and brought his lips to mine. He resisted at first, but he looked at me in my eyes and gave in. Our tongues danced for what seemed like eternity. I was finally able to catch my breath when he pulled away from our embrace.

"In a minute," he said as he turned to walk out the hospital room.

Stanley left the hospital, and I felt like I was on cloud ten. I rubbed my belly and smiled. *It was only a matter of time before we would be together and be a family,* I thought to myself. The thoughts of being in jail faded out of my mind. That was until there was a knock on the door, and a tall black man entered. His salt and pepper fade let me know that he was an older man. The badge he sported on his chest was enough to make my monitors go off. He wore a black suit, without the jacket, and he had a thick envelope tucked under his arms.

"Calm down, calm down, Ms. Gower. Don't be alarmed. I am just here to ask you some questions," he said as he sat down where Stanley had been sitting not too long ago. He extended his hand. "I'm Detective Lang. I'm working on your case."

My hand shook almost uncontrollably as I tried to shake his hand.

"Karisha," I spoke barely at a whisper.

"Nice to finally meet you, Karisha," he said, and his dimple popped out when he smiled at me. "So can you tell me

what happened at the baby shower of Latanya and Stanley?"
He got right to the point.

I didn't answer him right away; I was debating if I
should tell the truth or not.

"I already spoke with Latanya, by the way."

I guess that was his way of telling me that the truth
was what he came for.

"If you already spoke with her, then you know the
story."

I decided to just be honest. Stanley had my back. I was
going to jail regardless.

"So everything Latanya told me was the truth?" he
asked me before continuing. "There's nothing to add to it?" I
shook my head no. "Are you sure, Karisha? Once I turn over
my report, you will most likely be arrested and charged with
assault of a pregnant woman and possession of a deadly
weapon. You do understand that, right?" He asked, trying to
get me to talk.

"Yes, I understand. Are we done now?"

I just wanted him out of my face.

He took a deep breath and said, "Fine. Well, I'll be in
touch. You are to be released tomorrow. I'll be back to get you
then. You will be taken to L.A. County Jail to serve your time."

He stood to leave. "You can always contact me to give your statement," he added as he handed me his card on his way out.

The reality of everything hit me once I was alone in my hospital room. The tears began to cascade down my cheeks. There was no way around it: I was going to jail. Neither my family nor friends cared to check on me, not would they probably care that I was going to jail. At least I had Stanley.

Stanley was always there when I had nobody. I smiled at the thought of telling him I'm carrying his child. He loves me, so I know that the jail time didn't matter. We would be together sooner than later.

Averie

Tony had been blowing me up for two days now. I still didn't want to talk to him though. Every call got rejected, and I didn't bother to check any text messages or voicemails from him. He put his hands on me, even after he promised he wouldn't. I didn't understand how he could be so careless as to raise his hand to me after telling me how upset he was as a child from seeing his dad beat his mom. He most definitely picked up a few of his bad habits—the drugs that nobody knew about, the cheating and now the abuse.

I was on my way to my homegirl Mimi's house to have a few drinks and talk some shit when I remembered I needed to stop at a store to get my drink. Being as though I was on a side of the city that was unfamiliar to me, I was scared to go too far away from Mimi's house. I ain't from Compton and know next to nothing about the city. When I pulled up and parked in front of the liquor store, NATES, I was petrified. There were so many men in front of the store, just chilling and talking shit. I rolled my eyes as I took my key out of the ignition.

"Please, don't let one of these fools say anything crazy to me," I said to myself as I prepared to exit my car.

Before I even made it into the store, some old drunk ass man grabbed me by my elbow.

"Honey, can you spare some change?" he asked, displaying the yellowest teeth I've ever seen.

I snatched my arm away and said, "No, but if you grab me like you know me again, I'll spare an ass whooping."

I turned to walk away. I heard snickers as I walked into the store. The man behind the register, a big ole Mexican, blew me a kiss as I walked towards the back of the store to the wine. I stood in the middle of the aisle looking for the Stella Rosa Black I'd been craving. I saw it on the bottom shelf. When I bent down to get it, I felt someone brush past me. I instantly became livid.

"What the fuck?!" I yelled as I turned around ready to go off, but I lost my train of thought when I saw his face.

My eyes traveled up to his face, and my heart fluttered. His light brown eyes did something to me, the white T-shirt he wore was fresh as fuck, and his cut was fresh, too. The way he stood there like he didn't do nothing wrong was so sexy and enticing that it made me want to fuck him on sight, but that's not me. He stood and waited for me to say something else, like he knew he had me speechless. I just couldn't get over how his eyes looked through me. He smiled at me before I could say anything else, which really made weak.

"My bad, baby. I didn't mean to scare you. I was just trying to get past, and well, ya know."

He looked at me, implying that my ass was in the way. I still couldn't say anything back.

He extended his hand and said, "My name is Stan."

I accepted his handshake. "Averie."

I turned back around to pick up the bottle of Stella Rosa Black and started towards the counter to pay.

"It was nice meeting you, Averie." Stan said as I walked away from him.

On my way out of the store, I was still in lala land, basically floating all the way back to the car. I put the key in the ignition, and there was a knock on my window. I looked to my left to see who it was. I thought it was the bum from earlier asking for money, but it was Stan. He motioned for me to roll down my window. I rolled the window down.

"Yes?"

"I was wondering if I could take you out one day, Averie."

I chewed on my bottom lip, debating on whether I should be mean or nice to him.

"You don't have to answer me right now, but Imma need your number, so you can tell me later," he cracked a smile.

I chuckled. "So you think it's that easy, huh?" I asked him.

"Nah, not that easy, but I know you wanna give me your number. If you didn't, you wouldn't have rolled down your window, nor would you be talking to me still." He said matter-of-factly. He was right. His self-assurance had me grinning like a Cheshire cat.

"562-342-5544," I said as I took my car out of park and into drive. I backed up before he could even get off my window. "Talk to you later, Stan," I said as I drove off and could see him looking at me in my rearview.

Tony

"Hey, Tony, can you pick us up from the hospital today?"

I called Lala to see what she and Kamille were up to today. I knew they were being released today, and I wanted to see my baby. So when she asked me if I could pick them up from the hospital, I got a bit too excited.

"Yea. What time you gone be ready?"

"We should be ready at eleven. Can you stop by my mom's house and get the car seat?" she asked me.

I really didn't want to stop by her mom's house, though. I knew Stanley and his boys would most likely be out, and I didn't have time for their bullshit right now.

"How about I buy a car seat, you know, one to just keep with me, in my car?"

The line went silent for a minute.

"I mean, if you want to do that, then go ahead. I mean, you will have her, so that'll be smart," she replied.

My heart smiled.

"Okay. Well, I'll see y'all at eleven," I replied.

"Thank you, Tony."

"No problem."

I made my way to Babies "R" Us. I got the most expensive car seat. I read the back of the boxes, and I wanted the most protective car seat for my princess. I even got the mirrors that you put on the seat so you can see the baby as you drive.

When I got up to the counter to pay, the cashier asked, "First-born?"

"Yes," I blushed.

"Congrats, sir. You got all the right things."

I don't know why, but that brought me so much joy. I walked out of the store beaming. I packed the trunk and decided to set the car seat up. I wanted everything to be right for my baby girl. I smiled at myself when I finished putting the car seat in the car correctly. I got in the car and was about to drive off when my phone went off. "Averie" popped up on my screen. She finally decided to return my text, but now I didn't even care to read it. I put my phone down and put my car in drive. Wale blasted through my speakers. I turned up Black Cobain's part and rapped it with him.

Lala

I decided to call and ask Tony to pick Kamille and me up from the hospital when we were discharged. Stanley hadn't talked to me since yesterday, and I really didn't want to bother him. He knew Kamille wasn't his, so I knew he was hurting, even though he was trying to hide it. I felt like I was going to have a mental breakdown. I keep digging myself in deeper holes. The nurse walked in the room with a piece of paper in her hands. The way she looked at me, I knew it was the DNA results. I already knew the results. I didn't care to hear them, but she had to tell me.

"How are you today?" she asked as I pulled up my sweats.

"I'm fine," I replied as I sat down, winded. I looked at the paper she held. "Are those what I think they are?"

She looked and me and nodded.

She began to hand the paper to me, but I insisted, "No, you read it."

"Are you sure?" She asked as she took a seat in the chair next to the bed. "Okay love, well…" she paused. "It seems like Stanley is NOT the father of baby Kamille."

She didn't look surprised and neither did I.

"Yea, that was a given," I said.

"I know it's not my business, but I see the stress in your face, love. Do you have an idea as to who her father is?" she asked.

As if on cue, Tony walked through the door. Her attention went from me to the door where Tony stood.

"Oh, okay. Well, I'll let you guys pack up. I'll be back in a few with your discharge papers," she said as she walked past Tony and out of the room.

"What was that all about?" Tony asked as he walked in the room.

"DNA results for Stan and Kamille."

I had no reason to lie to Tony anymore, or so I thought.

"So what did they say?" he asked as he sat down across from me.

I gave him a "WTF?" look.

"Eh, they said what we already knew," I said as I reached down to pick up my Nikes.

"Hmmm, okay," he said.

That caught me off guard.

"What you mean 'Hmmm, okay'? You got something you want to say, Tony?" I asked him as I tied my shoe.

"Nah," he responded as he picked Kamille up out of her bed.

I turned my attention back to getting dressed so I could get Kamille dressed and be ready to leave by the time our nurse returned.

"Hand her here," I asked as I set out her clothes.

Tony walked over to me with Kamille in his arms. As he handed her over to me, he stopped and looked at her. Her eyes were wide open as if she knew who he was.

"Hi, baby girl," he sang as I laid her down on the sheets to change her. "So where am I taking you guys?" Tony asked me.

I hadn't thought about that, oddly. I didn't want Tony to take us to my mom's house because Stanley and Xavier would be around. I didn't want him to take me home because I didn't want to be alone, but I knew Stanley might be there too. But I for sure didn't want to go to his house. It was always nasty over there, and if I couldn't stand the smell when we were together, then I knew I couldn't handle it now.

"Ummm, just take me to LaShae's house."

He nodded, and I finished getting Kamille ready. As if on cue, the nurse walked in ready to discharge the two of us. After giving me my discharge instructions, she wheeled

Kamille and I downstairs to Tony's car, and we were on our way.

The car ride to LaShae's house was silent, to say the least. It's like we both wanted to say something but didn't know how. I was so lost in my own thoughts that I didn't notice the car stopped. I felt like I was digging myself in a deeper hole with everybody around me. All my lies would come to the light sooner or later, and I really didn't want to go through that aftermath. I'd already told Stanley that he wasn't Kamille's dad. Now I had Tony believing he was really her father, when in reality, there was a possibility that Xavier was Kamille's father as well.

"Tony, we need to talk," I finally spoke up before he could get out of the car to help me out.

"I figured that. What's wrong, La?"

He knew me too well. I always felt like he would read my mind and know exactly what was bothering me, but he would always let me tell him. I looked over at Kamille as she slept peacefully in her car seat.

"It's about the baby." He turned around in his seat to look at me. His eyes told me he already knew what I was going to say. "Tony, she might not be yours neither... I... I slept with..."

"Get the fuck out my car!" he yelled, stopping me midsentence and shocking the hell out of me.

"Huh," I asked because I thought maybe I was tripping.

"You heard me. Get the fuck out of my car! I knew it! I knew you didn't know! Blood, I fucking felt it!" he yelled at me. Tony began to beat the steering wheel and curse. "You stupid bitch! You knew it! I knew it! You fuckin' liar!"

He looked at me in the rearview mirror. He looked deranged. Almost immediately, I began to cry and shake. Tony never raised his voice at me. He got out the driver's seat and opened the back door as if he was really putting me out. I didn't know what to say; I knew there wasn't anything I could possibly say to make anything better.

I reached over to unlock the car seat, and he stopped me, "Bitch, please, I bought that. Leave it right there and get the fuck out."

He reached over me and grabbed Kamille's baby bag and threw it on the concrete.

"Have you lost your fucking mind? Don't ever throw my baby's stuff! I don't care how mad you are at..."

He punched me dead in my mouth before I could finish my sentence.

"Don't say shit to me! Don't ever fuckin' speak to me again!"

I screamed in agony. Kamille woke up out of her sleep screaming as well. I couldn't even react before he was pulling me out of his back seat and onto the ground. I had never seen this side of him before. Once I was on the ground, or should I say, out of the car, he unstrapped Kamille and handed her to me on the pavement.

"You ruined my fucking life, you stupid ass hoe! karma is a bitch!" he said before he got back in the car and pulled off.

"Tell me something I don't know," I said to myself as I sat on the concrete cradling and trying to calm my baby down.

I guess LaShae heard the commotion because she came running outside with my brother-in-law, Quincy.

"What the fuck!" LaShae yelled. "Who did this to you, La? What happened?"

"T...Tony, Tony got mad because I told him he might not be Kamille's dad," I made out through tears.

I was so ashamed. I didn't even want to repeat it. LaShae and Quincy looked at each other shocked.

"I thought Stanley was Kamille's daddy, La?" LaShae asked in a sincere voice as she tried to help me off the ground.

"Noooooooooo, we got a DNA test at the hosp...

hospital and it came back negative. He's not her dad."

I broke down in my sister's arms. Quincy took Kamille

from me and began walking in the house. I guess he figured

this was a conversation for sisters only.

"Latanya, what the fuck?! Why did you have THEM

believing they were her dad! Who is her dad, Lala?"

She looked at me trying to find the answer that I didn't

want to give.

I sniffled. "X." I finally admitted the truth to someone

other than myself.

Tony

As I made my way away from LaShae's house, I had to pull over because I felt sick to my stomach. Lala broke my heart. I thought after losing so much that I'd finally have something of my own: my baby. But she's not my baby; she belongs to another nigga. I felt betrayed, to say the least. I tried to think back to where I might've given Lala a reason to do me like this. Nothing I'd ever done to her could amount to the pain I felt right now. Only one thing was going to lessen the pain: a bottle. I started my car back up and made my way to the liquor store.

"Lemme get that bottle of Hennessy... Nah, the fifty-dollar bottle, blood," I told Hector as I stood in the liquor store.

"That's all for you, boss?" Hector asked.

"Yea, man." I put my money on the counter. "Keep the change," I said as I walked out of the store.

On my way to the house, I called up one of my old partners, Javi.

"Aye, man, you got some?" I asked into the receiver.

"Yea. How much you need, Tone?" he replied.

"Give me five grams of powder," I told him.

The phone conversation was silent for a few seconds.

"Powder? Man, what you goin' through? You sure you don't want no dro?"

Javi was aware of my battle with powder. A lot of people didn't even know I had a problem. Watching my mother get abused and then abuse herself with drugs, I had no choice but to experiment. I experimented a few times and started getting addicted. Javi was my supplier back then. He got me started, but he's also the one that got me off of the shit.

"I haven't relapsed in a few years, almost five, but this shit is too much, man. I need my nerves to be calmed down and back to normal. Yea, I want five grams. I'll come by in a minute to get it. Javi, don't give me no bullshit neither. I'm spending good money with you, Javi," I spoke into the phone.

He didn't reply right away. I know he didn't want to give it to me.

"Okay, come through." He let out a deep sigh before hanging up the phone.

When I arrived at the trap to pick up my order, Javi was reluctant to give it to me.

"Man, you sure?" he asked.

I knew I put him in a tough position, being a friend and a dealer, but he was about his money at the end of the day.

"Yea, blood, I'm good."

He handed me my baggy, and I was out of there as fast as I pulled up. On my way home, I thought about the last few months, shit, the last year. I tried to figure out where shit went sour. *When did shit get this bad?* Karma was really coming full circle for what I'd been doing in the dark. From cheating on Lala with my best friend, to meeting Averie, falling in love and losing her. I couldn't fucking win. *This couldn't be life,* I thought to myself as I drove home.

Averie

I didn't expect Stanley to remember my number. I mean, I gave it out real quick and pulled off, but somehow, he remembered it. When I pulled up to Mimi's house, that hoochie was on the porch waiting for me. I guess she thought I got lost. We drank and talked our shit, and I ended up stumbling out of there around midnight and made my way home. It wasn't until the next morning that I checked my phone and noticed that Stanley texted me and that I'd text Tony.

I slapped my forehead. "Damn! Always drunk texting."

I was scared to read what I'd sent him, so I deleted the message altogether.

Stanley was persistent. He texted me and asked if he could see me, and I told him I had to work. He said he didn't mind bringing me lunch, and with the hangover I was battling, I didn't mind the free food. I sat at my desk, antsy for hours. I didn't know if it was nerves from seeing him or my stomach just messing up because of all the wine I drank. I tried to do as much work as possible, but I couldn't concentrate. At 12:30 on the dot, my phone lit up with a message from Stanley.

"I'm outside."

Butterflies fluttered out of nowhere. I made my way to the restroom to fix myself.

"Okay, I'm coming," I replied.

I checked my gloss and fixed my hair before I went to meet him outside. The dress I wore hugged my hips just right. It was my favorite color dress, salmon. My salmon Aldo six-inch steppers, a name I affectionately called them, elongated my legs and made my ass sit up a little higher than normal. My breasts were sitting right, and although I felt like shit, I looked like a million bucks. I could tell Stan felt the same way when I saw the look on his face as I got off the elevator. He was in awe, mouth almost hanging. He had his cell up to his ear but told whoever he was talking to that he had to go.

I could smell the Jean-Paul Gaultier cologne he wore before we even embraced, and that shit made me weak.

"Mmmmmm, you smell good," I said as I let go of him.

He didn't let me go, and he commented, "You smell good, too...Dolce and Gabbana Light Blue?"

That turned me on even more, a man that knew his scents. I couldn't get Tony to care about cologne or perfume for shit. He was a regular AXE-wearing nigga.

"How'd you know?" I asked as I tried to pull away from him again, and this time he let me go.

35

He looked me up and down before he answered my question.

"I know my shit," was all he said.

"Hmph, so where's my food?" I asked as I stood with my hand my hip.

He laughed and said, "It's in the car, boo. Let's go."

I followed his lead. When we got out front, I didn't know which direction to go in being that I didn't see his car when I met him at the store. He walked over to a Mercedes-Benz S550, cream with butter brown seats. I looked at the car in awe, but I didn't want him to think I wasn't used to nice things, so I closed my mouth and waited patiently. He hit the alarm, and I heard the doors unlock. He walked over to the passenger side and opened the door. My homegirl was on her way back from lunch, and she stopped me.

"Girl, that's you?" she asked as she eyed the car and Stan.

"Girl, I don't know yet," I said as I gave her a five on the low.

"See ya upstairs, girl," she said as she walked into the building.

Stan returned from the car with a take-out bag from R&R's and a bouquet of roses. Never in my life had I received flowers from a man. The gesture brought tears to my eyes.

"What's wrong, boo?" he asked as he held the bag and roses in front of me.

"I....I've never gotten flowers from a man before." I was almost embarrassed to admit it.

"Awww, boo," he said as he came in to hug me. "You'll get all the flowers plus some more from this man, I promise."

He kissed me on my cheek. I broke our embrace and looked him in his eyes, searching for a lie or something, but couldn't find anything. I hugged him.

"Thank you, Stan," I whispered in his ear.

"No, thank you, beautiful. Now go eat and text me when you get off," he instructed then hugged me a little longer and then kissed my forehead.

I blushed.

"Okay. I'll talk to you later."

I turned to walk back into the building.

Stanley

I don't know if I was vulnerable, simping, or just really feeling Averie already. I just met her, and I felt something already. That kind of shit rarely happened to me; it was something about her. I left her job beaming with pride. Making my way back to the city from Cerritos where Averie worked, Nipsey's "4 in the Morning" blasted through my speakers. Instantly, thoughts of Karisha clouded my mind. The last time we spoke, she was on her way to jail. She refused to speak with detectives, and they weren't about to play with her, so they threw her crazy ass in the county. Knowing what kind of bitch Karisha is, that shit wasn't nothing to her. Bitches like that pride themselves on taking cases for niggas and shit. I can't knock her for that; that's part of the reason I fuck with her. I feel like I owe her that much. I led her on because I knew I didn't want any relationship with her. She tried to kill my girl, the one girl that I really loved, yet I still fucked with her. I honestly feel like a bitch ass nigga. My side bitch had more control over my life than I did.

When I pulled up on the block, X and Rag were sitting in X's garage. I honked at them and parked in front of my mom's house. I noticed Sheila's car parked in the driveway. I haven't seen or heard from her in a few months since she found out Lala was pregnant. She'd been acting stupid and keeping Shi'ann away from me. She refused to let me see my baby, and that pissed me off because I actually take care of mine. Bitch will call asking for money, but I can't see my baby? *The nerve of these bitches,* I thought to myself as I parked my car. Shi'ann came running out of the house with my mom on her heels.

"Shi'ann, girl, slow down," my mom yelled after her while Shi'ann tried to skip a few steps coming off the porch.

I ran and caught her right before she was able to fall and hurt herself.

"Dadddddyyyyy," she sang as she hugged my neck.

"How's daddy's baby?" I asked as I lifted her off her feet. She held on to my neck for dear life. "I missed you, baby," I told her as I looked at her and held her in my arms.

I hugged her tight as hell. The whole Lala thing really had me feeling some type of way. It made me appreciate my baby so much more.

"Stan, we need to talk," Sheila's voice snapped me back to reality.

I couldn't help but snarl at her when I looked up.

"Nah, we don't. I tried to talk. You can leave. I'll bring her home later."

I tried to walk past her and go in the house. My mom must have read my body language because she grabbed Shi'ann out of my arms and walked her back towards the front door.

"Come on, baby. You can help nana in the kitchen," she said as she walked through the screen door.

"I'll be in there in a minute, Shi," I said before turning my attention back to Sheila. "What you wanna talk about, man?" I asked as I sat on the top step.

She stood in front of me with her hand on her hip.

"How's your baby? I heard she had her." Her tone was sarcastic, and it pissed me off.

I gave her the side eye and said, "Man, we can talk about Shi, or you can get the fuck out of my face."

I reached for my vibrating phone in my pocket. Pulling it out, the screen read a Global Tel Link number. *Karisha,* I thought to myself. I declined the call and slid my phone back in my pocket. When I looked up, Sheila was shooting daggers with her eyes. I knew she was really mad because the thought of me starting a family with someone else was always her biggest fear, even if she was slutting around while I tried to do that with her.

"Okay, you don't have anything to say. I'll drop Shi'ann off at your mom's house later or in the morning," I told her before I stood up to walk in the house.

"You must've found out she ain't yours," she snickered. I stopped in my tracks.

"What you say?" I asked her.

"You heard me. You must've found out that bitch baby ain't yours. She had yo' ass fooled."

Now she flat out laughed in my face. My reflexes mixed with my embarrassment and emotions made me backhand her. As she took a few steps backward, trying to catch herself from falling, she felt her face and noticed blood on her hand. She looked up at me and came charging at me. Her arms were flying wild and fast. She was clearly trying knock my head off my shoulders, and she finally caught me with a good one to my mouth. I had to step back and grab my mouth. I went forward, but not to hit her. I tried to grab her arms because he she would have hit me again. I would have forgotten she was my baby momma.

.

Hearing the commotion, my mom came running out the front door. X and Rag made their way across the street too.

"You dumb bitch ass nigga! Don't ever fucking think you can touch me! I ain't one of these young bitches out here. You know better, bitch!" she spat as my mom tried to pull her away.

"Hush, chile! Shi'ann is going to hear y'all! Y'all want her to see this shit?" My mom looked from me to Sheila and back.

Sheila was furious though.

"Nah, fuck that! He hit me!"

She pushed my mom out the way and tried to run up on me again, but this time X grabbed her and lifted her off the ground.

"Sheila, stop before..." I started to say, but she cut me off.

"Before you what, bitch?!"

She caught me off guard with the word "bitch." She knew better. My mom and X tried to calm her down and get her in the car while Rag asked me what happened.

Before I could respond, Sheila yelled over everyone, "Fuck you, Stanley! Abusive punk ass nigga! That's why that baby ain't yours! The whole hood laughing at yo ass because they know what's up!" She turned around pointing at X and Rag. X and Rag looked at each other then back at me. "Bitch ass nigga," she spat before she pulled off.

"Stanley, what the hell was that about?" my mom asked as she walked back to the porch.

X and Rag walked up, too.

This time she yelled. "You hear me talking to you, Stanley!"

"She talks too fucking much, and she hit me first," I lied. Truth was Sheila hit a nerve that I thought nobody else knew about. I turned my attention back to X and Rag. " You knew?" I asked them.

"Man, I don't know what that bitch is saying. I'm sorry, moms. I don't know what that girl is talking about," Rag replied while X just stood there.

"X, you knew?"

My mom looked at us crazy.

"Knew what? What they 'pose to know, Stan?" she inquired.

"Lala baby ain't mine, damn!"

I was angry now. X still didn't reply. He just stood and didn't say anything. I couldn't believe this shit. "Cuh, get the fuck out my yard," I spat at X and Rag as I turned to walk in the house with my confused mother on my heels.

When I got in the house, I plopped down on the couch in the den. Shi'ann was still in the kitchen mixing things. My mom walked over and sat down next to me. Chocolate smooth skin and big beautiful eyes. I could see the worry in her face.

"I'm okay, mom," I told her.

She grabbed my chin, "No, you not, Stan. You forget I'm your momma. I had you, I raised you, and I know when something's wrong. So what happened?" She asked me.

I know men aren't supposed to cry, but I broke down right there in front of my mom.

"The baby ain't mine. It's her ex-boyfriend baby."

I hadn't told anybody that shit; it was embarrassing. My phone vibrated in my pocket again. I pulled it out, and of course, it was Karisha. I answered this time and pressed seven.

Before she could say anything, I spoke, "Stop calling my damn phone. I'll put money on your books every month until you get out, but I ain't fucking with you no more. Leave me the fuck alone," then I hung up the phone. My mom looked stunned. "That wasn't nobody, mom," I told her before she could ask.

"I'm still stuck on that not being your baby, but then again, Stanley, I always tell you that Karma is a bitch," she said as she patted me on my leg and got up from the couch.

Karma was indeed being a bitch.

Karisha

"In the case of Karisha Gower vs. the People of the State of California, we the jury, find Karisha, GUILTY of all charges."

My heart sank as they read the verdict. I knew I was going to go and be in jail for a little while, but to actually hear them say "Guilty" made the shit hit home. I looked around the courtroom, and I didn't see anyone I knew. Not even Stanley. I walked out of the courtroom with my head hanging low. I'll be spending the next seven years in this muthafucka. *Seven years in jail.* I shook my head at myself. *I wouldn't even get to be with my baby*, I thought as we rode back to jail from court. I got back to the jail and was able to make a phone call.

I called Stanley. I was finally ready to tell him about the baby. The first time it went to voicemail, but the second time he answered. Even though I was mad that he didn't show up, I still was happy that he answered the phone, but I was in for a big surprise. He told me to leave him alone and to stop calling his phone. I looked at the receiver like it was tripping. I tried to speak, but the phone line was already dead.

I would be serving seven years with not one friend or family member, nor the man that I love, by my side. I couldn't believe my life really turned into this piece of shit. Anger burned through my veins as I laid in bed that night recalling what Stanley said. How dare he? He thought it was cool because he said he was gonna put money on my books until I was released, but what the fuck was I supposed to do in between time? Who was going to take care of our child? I got up from my cot and went back to the phone.

I dialed Stanley's number, but this time it was a recording. He'd blocked my calls. I shook uncontrollably; my heart literally broke into pieces right there at that pay phone. *Fuck Stanley*, I thought. I did so much for him and look at me being forgotten and blocked. The nerve of that bitch ass nigga. I shoulda killed him when I tried to kill Lala, but his time is coming. *Seven years ain't shit to a bitch with a plan*, I thought as I laid in my cot with a wicked smile.

My presence will be felt when I get out. Believe that. My thoughts trailed off into thoughts of motherhood. My eyes watered from the reality that I'd spend my pregnancy behind bars. I would deliver my baby shackled to a hospital bed. I turned over and cried into my pillow.

Tony

The powder hit me hard as hell when I sniffed my first line. My nostrils burned, but I didn't care. I took a shot of my drank and sniffed another fat ass line. I threw my head back and exhaled. My heart was beating so fast. I just wanted to numb all the pain and the thoughts. As I held my head back, thoughts of Lala and Kamille clouded my mind. I thought back to how I did Lala that day. I had never hit her, but she deserved it this time. She knew I wasn't the baby daddy, just like she knew Stanley wasn't. She had the victim role down pat.

I thought about Averie. I missed her, and she haven't answered none of my calls. When she did return the call, I missed it, thanks to Lala. Now when I called, it went straight to voicemail. A part of me knew she was moving on with her life because that's just how Averie is. She's about her business, she doesn't stay hung up on one thing too long, and I don't blame her, because, well, look what happened to me. I needed to talk to her, though, so I decided to write a letter. I took another shot and grabbed my notebook off the coffee table and started writing:

Dear Averie,

I miss you, man. I know I was wrong, and I hurt you, but I miss you. It was dumb of me to leave you hanging over someone who always left me hanging, and I'm sorry. I'm sitting here drinking and sniffing lines. Yes, I sniffed a few lines. Before all of this, I'd been able to control my drug use, 'cause you were my drug. I didn't need this shit when you were with me. Baby, I'm sorry. Just come back to me. I don't have nobody. Lala lied to me; that ain't my baby. She played all of us. Averie, I'm sorry. Please come back.

Love you,

Tony

I dropped my pen on the table and sniffed the last two lines off the glass. I could feel my heart beating through my chest, I felt funny. I laid my head back and tried to calm myself down, but I couldn't. I felt myself dozing off. I didn't fight it; I embraced it. I never would've thought I was embracing death.

Lala

2 weeks later

I've been staying in LaShae's spare bedroom since Tony whooped my ass and kicked me out the car that day. I thought about those moments every day, and I still couldn't believe he did that with my baby in my arms. Kamille was just three days old at the time. I prayed that she wouldn't remember any of it. I rarely came out of my room since I'd been staying with my sister. Calling it embarrassment was an understatement; I really didn't know what to say to anyone. I hated that Quincy and LaShae had to see me like that, but I'm very grateful that they opened up their doors for Kamille and me. I could've gone back to the apartment Stanley, and I shared, but I chose not to because I didn't want to run into him.

"Lala, you gotta come out of hiding," LaShae said as she opened the blinds in the room.

The sun was shining so bright, and my eyes had to adjust.

"I don't have anywhere to go, and I'm not hiding," I said as I rolled over and covered my head.

I felt LaShae sit on the edge of the bed. She had Kamille in her arms. She rarely didn't have Kamille in her arms these days.

"You are going to spoil my baby," I said.

LaShae snatched the cover off of me and said, "Look at your mommy, Kamille. She looks so bummy," she chuckled.

We chuckled. That was the first time I'd laughed since the whole thing with Tony. There was a knock on the door, and we both looked up to see Quincy standing there.

"Lala, you have a visitor."

I looked him like he was crazy.

"A visitor?" I asked. "Who knows I'm here?" I looked at LaShae, who was trying to avoid eye contact. "LaShae!!!!"

I kicked her in her butt. I almost kicked her off the bed until I realized she was still holding my baby.

"I went to momma house the other day, and he asked about you," she said all nonchalant.

"He! Who is he?!" I stood up from the bed.

"Xavier," Quincy chimed in with a smile.

I don't know who I wanted to hit more, LaShae for telling him to come over or Quincy for letting him in.

"I'm not even dressed! I look a mess and look at my face."

51

I pointed out the fact that my lip was still swollen and bruised, even though it was two weeks later. Tony really did a number on my face.

"Girl, go take a shower and get dressed. You know he don't mind waiting," LaShae said as she left the room with Kamille and Quincy in tow.

I sat back down on the bed and thought about what I would say to Xavier. I hadn't talked to him since the day I was released, and I didn't know how he really felt. I knew Xavier had feelings for me, but I didn't know if they were like the ones I had for him.

I finally got up and showered. I stood under the warm water for as long as I could, I didn't want him waiting too much longer. Wale's "Passive-Aggres-Her" played as I got dressed in front of the big mirror in my room. My body snapped right back to normal after I had Kamille; I reminded myself to thank my mom for good genes. I finally got the hips and booty I envied LaShae for having. I smiled at my reflection. It's been so long since I actually smiled a real smile. Thank God LaShae stopped by my apartment the other day to pick up some clothes for Kamille and me. All I wanted to wear were sweats lately. I think it's because that's all I wore my last month of being pregnant; the comfort was what I was looking for. Especially at a time like this.

Dressed in a pair of Hollister sweats and a beater, I finally made my way downstairs.

"Dang, finally," Quincy said as I walked down the stairs.

"Oh, shut up!" I nudged him in his side as I walked by him to get to Xavier.

Xavier's eyes lit up when he saw me. He tried to hide his smile, but his dimples gave it away as they peeked out. He held Kamille in his arms with his chest poked out.

"Pictures don't do her any justice, La," he said as he walked over and embraced me.

A part of me didn't want to let him go, but I did.

"You look good, La... What happened to your face?" Xavier asked in a worried tone when he finally noticed it.

I put my head down out of shame.

"Tell him, La!" LaShae's nosey ass yelled from the kitchen.

"Tell me what? What happened to you?" X raised his voice a little bit, not too loud because he didn't want to scare Kamille.

"Tony hit me," I whispered with my head still down.

Xavier got up from the couch and walked over to where Kamille's swing was and put her in it.

"Tony did *what*?" He asked as he walked back over to me. His anger began to rise.

"He hit me," I replied.

"No! He fucked her up! And then kicked her out of the car with Kamille in her arms," LaShae answered for me.

LaShae talks entirely too much. I shot her a stank look like "STFU."

"He hit you, Lala?" Xavier asked as he lifted my head up by my chin.

I couldn't even look him in his eyes to tell him the truth because I was afraid that he would ask why.

"Yes, he beat me up and threw me out of his car because I told him that he wasn't Kamille's dad."

I dropped my head again in embarrassment. When Xavier stepped up to embrace me, I jumped. I guess you can say my nerves weren't so good. PTSD, I guess. He hugged me tight.

"La, I'm sorry all of this is happening to you," he said as he held me in his arms.

For the first time since being beat up, I let out my tears. I cried so hard my body shook. I was mentally, physically and emotionally drained, and I could only blame myself for it. Xavier held me for what seemed like forever before he sat down on the couch.

"We'll let you two talk," LaShae and Quincy said as they took Kamille towards the back of the house.

"You good?" Xavier asked.

When I looked up, and my eyes met his, I felt faint. The look in his eyes was a look of love and compassion, something I hadn't seen in a while. I saw lust in Stanley's eyes when he looked at me, even though he swore he loved me.

"Yea, X, I'm good."

I sat up and tried to wipe my face. Xavier grabbed my hands and put them back in my lap and put his arm around my shoulder, pulling me in close to his chest.

"Don't hide your tears from me. I understand them," he said almost above a whisper.

I laid there with my head on his chest until I fell asleep. I didn't even know I fell asleep until I felt Xavier pick me up and walk me down the hall. Once inside the room, Xavier laid me on the bed and took off my sweats before putting the comforter over me.

"Kamille?" I asked for my baby.

"Wait a minute. They 'bout to bring her in here."

As if on cue, Quincy walked in cradling Kamille.

"Here ya go," he said as he handed her to Xavier.

Xavier nodded at Quincy, and he turned around to walk out the door. I laid on my side and watched Xavier say his goodbyes to Kamille. He gave her an Eskimo kiss and whispered something in her ear.

"Okay, La, Imma bounce," he said as he walked over to her bassinette and laid her down softly.

I sat up in the bed and answered, "Okay, thank you for coming to see us, Xavier. I really enjoyed your company."

"I'll be back, La. I promise."

He walked over to me and gave me the softest most sincere kiss on my lips. My body felt weak; I so desperately wanted him. I grabbed his arm as he tried to walk away. He looked down at me and smiled.

"You know it's too soon, La. Go to bed," he smiled and walked out the door, closing it behind him.

I lay on my back and smiled at the thoughts that already turned into sweet memories.

With Xavier, I was always happy. I always smiled when I was in his presence. I hardly ever felt like that around Stanley anymore. There was always tension when we were in each other's company. It was really sad. I daydreamed about my future with Xavier. I couldn't wait to get away from here and live our lives. We could never live together freely anywhere near Stanley's psycho jealous ass.

Our time was coming, though; I could feel it.

Averie

"Ahhhhh! Yesss, Daddy. Yesss," I said as I held my ass cheeks apart so Stanley could go deeper. "Yessssssss," he held my waist and pounded me from the back.

He started slowing down and going deeper, causing me to squirt a little bit.

"Yeaaaaa, squirt for daddy, baby...Yessss." He smacked my ass as I tried to throw it back on his dick.

Stanley's dick wasn't the biggest, but the nigga had a death stroke for sure. The way his dick hit the spots that ain't never been touched by another man, it drove me crazy.

"Ok, get on top. C'mon," he was out of breath. His fat ass was tired.

As he laid down on his back, I began straddling him, but I decided against it. I slid down his body until my head was at his abdomen. His dick was hard as a rock, sticking straight up in the air. I took it in my hand, gave it a little squeeze, and licked the tip. I felt his leg shake. I licked around the tip again before taking him into my mouth. Up and down, I stroked his dick while I sucked it. The warmth of my saliva drove him crazy; I could tell because he grabbed my head, slamming my mouth further and further down on his dick. I gagged, and he pushed my head down again. I felt my eyes watering as he fucked my face. Putting my hands on his waist, I started sucking the shit out of his dick. Spit dripped everywhere as I attempted to lick his balls.

"Yesssssss, babyyyyyyy. Yessss." Very safe to say he enjoyed the fellatio.

I raised my head and held on to his dick while I straddled it. I sat down slowly as Stanley's hands were planted on my waist. He pulled me down a little bit at a time. He knew this was teasing me. I moved his hands and slammed down on his dick and grinded.

"Ahhhh," he moaned as I grinded on his dick. "Kiss me," he said as I rode.

I went in for a kiss, and he held me as he started pumping in and out of me. I couldn't even concentrate on the kiss anymore; the dick felt too good.

"ZzzzZZZZzZzzz."

The room lit up as my phone vibrated on the nightstand. Stanley looked over in the direction of the light and looked at me.

"Ignore it," I said as I began grinding on him again.

He played with my nipples as I sat on top of him.

"Cum all over this dick, baby."

My pussy got wetter from that shit. I went harder and faster until I felt my orgasm approaching.

"I'm bout to cummmmmmmmmm," I said as he held on to my waist, guiding me on his dick.

"Yesssssssssss," he grunted. Then I felt the best feeling ever.

"Ahhhhhhhhhhhhhhhhhhhhhhhhhhhhhhhhhhhhhhhh," was all I could say as he bust inside of me and made me bust.

I laid there on top of him, panting, trying to catch my breath as he kissed my forehead.

"ZzzzzzzzzzzzzZZZzzZ."

The room lit up again as my phone vibrated. Stanley sighed and rolled over so that he was on top of me. He stroked me with his semi erect dick.

"Somebody tryna get in touch with you," his eyes lead me to my cellphone.

I tightened my muscles around his dick and tried to kiss him, but he moved his face.

"Who calling you this late?" he asked as he went deeper.

My chin lifted as I tried to talk, but I couldn't.

"..........I.... don't...don't... knowwww," I grabbed his face and made him kiss me.

His tongue explored my mouth, and his tongue made promises his dick was keeping. I felt his body tense up as he sucked on my neck.

"Cum for me, daddy," I whispered and rubbed his back as I felt him erupt again.

He took a deep breath and fell on top of me.

"That pussy bomb as fuck," he said as he rolled over, pulling his dick out of me.

"Thank you," I said as I kissed him and got out of the bed.

I was heading to bathroom, so I stopped and picked up my phone. I walked into the bathroom and sat down on the toilet. Peeing after sex was always hard for me to do, but fuck a UTI. I REFUSE! I sat there as I waited for the pee to find its way. Scrolling down my call log, I noticed the number that had called me twice was an unknown number. It was a 310 number that I had never seen before. I redialed the number, and a woman answered the phone.

"Hi, umm, did someone call Averie?" I spoke into the phone.

I could hear people talking in the background, unable to make out what they were saying. The lady that answered finally replied, "Yes, I did. This is Bridgette."

"I don't know a Bridgette. I think you might have the wrong number."

I was about to hang up when she said, "You know my son, Tony."

The line went quiet, a few seconds later I said, "Yes."

"Ummm hmmm, okay well. I found your number in his phone, and he left you a letter." She said.

I was confused, "Left me a letter? Where'd he go?"

She paused again, this time I could hear her sniffle as she answered, "He's dead...he overdosed two weeks ago. The police just found his body this morning."

She finally broke down. I didn't know what to do; I couldn't think or breathe. My hands shook. My legs trembled. Thank God I was sitting on the toilet or else I would have fallen.

"Oh my Godddddddddddddddddddddddddddddddddddd!!!" I yelled on accident. "No, nooo, nooo, nooo, nooo, noo!! He just called me. I should've answered! I was supposed to always answer."

The guilt I felt ate away at me like leeches.

"Baby, there's nothing you could have done. Tony had been fighting this battle for a long time. He hid his stress and worries well, baby. It's not your fault."

I forgot his mom was still on the phone. I tried to calm down as she spoke to me, but I couldn't. I hung up the phone and laid on the bathroom floor in fetal position, weeping. How selfish had I become? *I'm sitting up here fucking on another nigga, and the one that needed me, really needed me, had reached out to me, but I wasn't anywhere to be found,* I thought to myself as I wept.

There was a knock on the bathroom door a few minutes later; I totally forgot I'd left him in the bed.

"Averie?" He knocked again quietly. "Are you okay?" He slowly turned the doorknob and opened the door. When he walked in, he saw me lying on the ground and kneeled down to look at me. "Baby, what's wrong? Why are you crying?" he asked as he rubbed my head.

I couldn't say anything. I couldn't find the words. I just wanted Tony's mom to call back and say it was a mistake, that he was playing a prank on us.

"Averie, talk to me! What happened?!" Stanley asked and looked at me with sincere eyes.

"Mmmmmy...my ex died." I broke down again.

The look on Stanley's face changed from sincere to almost angry.

"What you say?" he asked as he looked at me.

The tears wouldn't stop. "My ex-boyfriend died, h...heee overdosed two weeks ago. His mom just ca... called mee."

"Baby, it's not your fault. There's nothing you could have done, " he soothed and rubbed my face again, but I could tell he was upset.

"I know...it's just that... he called, and I ignored it... his mom said he left me a letter."

"C'mon, get up from there," Stanley said as he stood me up. "It's gonna be okay, Averie. I'm here for you. I got you." He hugged me tight; my breast pressed against his chest. "What was his name?" Stanley asked.

It pained me to even say it because I didn't want to believe he was really gone.

"His name was Tony," I sobbed.

Stanley

Tony, I thought to myself. I know Tony is a common name, but Averie saying the name caught my attention.

"It's going to be okay, babe. Let's go get back in the bed."

I helped her to the bedroom. As she snuggled under me, I couldn't get Tony's face out of my mind. I'm not totally sure she was talking about the same dude, and I didn't want to alert her by asking too many questions. I laid with Averie until she cried herself to sleep and then I got up and went to the living room. I sat down on my leather lazy boy and unlocked my cell phone. I had a few messages, no missed calls, but of course, a bunch of alerts on Twitter and Instagram.

When I clicked on the Instagram app, the first picture that popped up was Tony's. My eyes almost popped out of my head; I couldn't believe it. The caption read, "RIP, my nigga Tone. Blood was cool people. Prayers going up for your fam." Something in me wanted to feel bad for the nigga, but I couldn't. I felt no remorse for his situation. A part of me was secretly happy because I knew it would hurt Lala if she found out he was dead. She'll eventually come crawling back because Kamille no longer had a father figure.

I continued scrolling down my newsfeed when I came across another picture that caught my eye. Xavier hardly ever dealt with social media, and he barely ever posted pictures on Instagram. When he did post a picture though, it was usually of his daughter, Tia. I guess he was feeling himself tonight because he posted his WCW later than everyone else. While examining the photo, my stomach began twisting in knots. The caption read: "My baby momma harder than a lot of you niggas." It wasn't a full-body picture. It was a female from the back. She wasn't skinny, but she wasn't fat neither. Her chocolate skin looked flawless, and the black cat tattooed on her lower back gave her away. I almost crushed my phone with my bare hands. I couldn't believe this shit. *Homies ain't homies no more,* I thought to myself as I locked my phone and headed back in the bedroom to Averie. I woke her outta her sleep, and I took out my frustration and anger on her pussy.

Averie

Stanley woke me up and fucked me harder than I'd ever been fucked before. I don't know if I felt love or hate while he was stroking me. I could tell that something was on his mind; he had this look in his eyes. I can't explain it, but it was a look I'd never seen before. After he came inside of me, he rolled over and went to sleep. I wrapped my arms around myself since that was the only comfort I was going to get in that bed. I dreamt of Tony. He was so real in my dream. I got to talk to him, explain to him why I did what I did and how I ended up with another man. He didn't say anything back to me; he just stared at me. I woke up to Stanley nudging me.

"Averie, wake up," he nudged me.

"I'm up. I'm up." I opened my eyes to see him sitting at the edge of the bed. "What's wrong?" I asked as I covered my mouth; morning breath is not cute.

"You was saying cuz name in your sleep. You dreaming about that nigga?" he asked with a look of disgust on his face.

"You act as if I didn't just find out he died, Stan!"

I got up from the bed. I didn't need this inconsiderate shit right now. I found my slacks that I had on the day before, and I slipped my blazer over my wife beater.

"I'll see you later," I said to Stanley as I walked out of the bedroom.

He followed me into the living room.

"Where you going?"

"I'm going home. I don't need your jealousy right now," I replied as I grabbed my keys and purse off the bar.

"Jealousy?" he asked. "You think I'm jealous because you said your dead ass ex-boyfriend name in your sleep?"

My mouth hung open because I couldn't believe he had the audacity to say some heartless shit like that to me.

"Yea, Imma just talk to you later, Stanley."

I slammed the door on my way out. Once inside my car, I broke down. I couldn't stop the tears if I wanted to. What was I doing? Tony would never talk to me like that. He wouldn't say most of the things Stanley thought it was okay to say. My heart broke into pieces as I thought about what I was doing two weeks ago and why I wasn't there for Tony. Still too emotional to start up my car, I sat in the driver's seat and just let the tears fall.

"Tony, I am so sorry," I spoke into the air. "I know you can hear me. I am so sorry. You didn't deserve it. Please forgive me."

I started up my car and made my way home. The drive home usually took about thirty minutes coming from Stanley's place, but today it took twenty at the most. I rushed inside my apartment, stripping out of my clothes as I walked around. I walked into my bedroom and took out a sweat suit and my Nike slippers. I let the shower warm up while I checked my mail. Bills, bills, bills, bills. *It's like a damn Destiny's Child song.* Throwing the envelopes to the side, I got in the shower. The hot water felt so good hitting my skin. I stood with my back to the water and let it ease all my stress and pain. Again, Tony popped in my head. The visual of him made me cry. He was really gone. I couldn't let myself believe it.

After washing myself, I stepped out of the shower and wrapped myself in a towel. There was a knock at my door. I looked toward the front door. Nobody knew I was home. I would usually be at work around this time. There was another knock, so I walked in my room to get my robe.

"Who is it?" I asked as I approached the door.

Whoever it was didn't respond. I looked out of the peephole, and from the back of his head, I knew exactly who it was. I unlocked and opened the door.

"What do you want, Stanley?" I asked with one hand on my hip.

He looked me up and down, something that would usually turn me on but not today.

"We need to talk, Averie," he said as he made his way past me, into the apartment.

"Come in please," I said sarcastically.

"Averie, I didn't mean to come off like I didn't care this morning. It was just weird for you to be crying a nigga name in your sleep."

The look on his face was sincere, but wrong was wrong, and he knew he was wrong.

"Okay," was all I said to him as I walked back to my room.

I sat down at the edge of my bed and began putting on my lotions. I rubbed the vanilla-scented lotion on my thighs and calves.

Stanley walked in and asked, "You need help?"

"No, I'm good," I said as I ignored his pervish smirk.

He sat down next to me and tried to touch my thigh. I popped his hand.

"Stanley, this isn't about to happen. I'm bout to get dressed and go pay my condolences. You came over here to apologize. Cool, I appreciate it, but if that's all, you can leave."

He looked at me like I had shit on my face.

"Fasho," was all he said as he stood to leave.

Once Stanley was out of my apartment, I got dressed and threw my hair in a messy ponytail. I mentally prepared myself for what I was about to walk into as I drove to Tony's mom's house on the Eastside of Compton. When I pulled up, there were a few cars parked in front of the house. I silently said a prayer as I got out of the car. Walking up the front porch, I spoke to family members, and hugged a few that I knew. I was reluctant to walk in the house. I could feel my eyes burning already. When I walked through the door, I was greeted by Tony's mom, Bridgette.

"Hi Ms. Bridgette," I reached out and hugged her as she stood near the kitchen.

"Hey, Averie baby….How are you?" She asked.

I really didn't know how to answer that question.

"I've had better days, but I'm here," I answered and tried to give her a smile.

"I understand, baby. Here, here's the letter." She reached in her pocket and pulled out the folded piece of paper. "I didn't read it. I felt like it was just for you," she said as she handed me the paper.

"Thank you," I whispered because my voice cracked with pain.

"You can go in Tony's old room and read it, baby," she said as she pointed down the hallway.

"Thank you."

I finally let the tears fall down my face.

Pictures down the hallway showed Tony as a newborn and throughout his youth and teenage years. I stopped at one picture. It was my favorite picture of Tony. He was in college; it was his football picture. He loved football. His smile was so beautiful and full of life. I touched his face and closed my eyes, wishing he would appear right here, right now. I opened the door to the room. It looked like it was the same way Tony left it when he left home. I sat on the twin size bed and rubbed my hand across the quilt that covered the mattress. I could still smell his scent in his pillows and comforter. Wiping my eyes, I opened the letter and began reading. My heart sank, my hands shook, and I cried uncontrollably.

"THAT BITCH!!!" I screamed.

I couldn't control my tears anymore. I re-read the sentences of the letter over and over again. My eyeball burned, and so did my nostrils. My hands shook violently as I balled up the piece of paper.

I closed Tony's bedroom door as I walked out of the room. Making my way down the hallway, trying to avoid looking at his pictures on the walls, I walked into the kitchen to find his mom.

"I am so sorry for your loss, Ms. Bridgette," I said, and I tried to hold in my tears.

"It's okay baby. He's in a better place now. No more pain and no more worries," she assured me as she hugged me.

I kissed her cheek and told her I would be back this week to check on her.

"Call me if you need anything," I told her as I turned to walk out of the house.

I ran into the chest of a woman. When I looked up to see who it was, my anger rose again.

"What the fuck are you doing here?" she asked me.

It was Terri, Tony's "best friend" that was in love with him. She was an Amazon. Freakishly large bitch. She stood about 5'9" and was thick. Like the real kind of thick. Her thighs were at least two of mine, and she had a permanent arch in her back. I knew from the first time I saw her why Tony made her his best friend. The bitch had ass, hips and, if she didn't talk, she was a pretty girl. She just felt some type of entitlement over Tony. I never liked their friendship. I didn't really respect it. But out of respect for my man, I respected her. He was no longer here though, so all that faux respect flew straight out the window.

"I should be asking you the same thing," I spat back at her.

Ms. Bridgette walked between us. "C'mon, you two. I don't need this right now."

"I'm leaving, Ms. Bridgette. Remember to call me if you need anything," I said as I began walking around Terri.

Terri stepped in my way, so I asked, "What is your problem?"

"You don't need to come back around here. You probably the reason Tony killed himself. You fucking left him hanging when he needed you," she said this shit like she knew our lives.

"You sure? Or is that the bullshit he fed you?" I asked.

Ms. Bridgette jumped in. "Terri, let it go. Just be quiet. Don't come over here starting shit."

"Okay. Imma let it go, but know this: you left him, and he came to me. He always came back to me. Nights when you thought he was working, he was with me. That was *my* man, and I'm carrying his child."

There was silence in the room as the words registered in my brain. *Carrying his child?* Is that what she just said? I looked at Terri. She had a smirk on her face. I looked down to her stomach, and she did indeed have a pouch. I felt nauseated. If I had eaten anything, I'm sure it would've came up right there.

"Terri, you are messy as hell! You couldn't wait to tell her that shit!" Ms. Bridgette scolded her.

I looked at Ms. Bridgette, asking, "You knew about this? Did Tony know?"

As tears filled my eyes, she answered, "I did know, baby. Tony didn't know yet though. She came over her crying to me. She wasn't sure if she was going to keep it...," her words trailed off as I zoned out.

I turned to walk out the door. I had to get away from Terri and Ms. Bridgette. I was sick to my stomach. Too much had been revealed. Tony killed himself because he wasn't Lala's baby daddy, and now Terri was carrying Tony's child. I sat in my car and cried. I couldn't even drive off. Terri walked outside after me, sporting a huge grin. She really thought she won a prize, but in reality, she had just been dealt some of the worst cards. She didn't realize how hard it would be to raise a child without its father around or alive. I said a silent prayer for her and one for myself as I headed to Stanley's to tell him about what I'd just found out. Hopefully, this time he would be considerate of my feelings and show a little compassion.

Stanley

When I left Averie's house, I made a mental note to treat her like shit whenever she decided she wanted to be bothered. I knew where she was headed, and that pissed me off even more. Why was a dead nigga that she no longer dealt with getting so much of her time? I pulled up in front of my mom's house. For months, I'd been trying to catch Lala while she was at her mom's house, and today I finally succeeded. I noticed Lala's car and LaShae's car parked in the long driveway of their house. I got out of the car and started making my way towards the house, but my mom called me before I could make it any further than my car door.

"Stanley, come here."

She stood on the porch with her hands on her hip. *What I do now?* I thought to myself as I made my way in the house.

"Mmmm, what's that smell, momma?" I asked as I walked into the kitchen and peaked under the lid of a pot. It was greens and cabbage mixed. My stomach immediately got happy. "I came over on the right day huh?" I asked with a smile on my face.

My smile faded when I turned to see her face, and it wasn't a happy face. She held a stack of envelopes in her hand.

"You need to tell your girls to send mail to YOUR HOUSE, NOT MINE!"

She threw the stack on the table. I picked up one and immediately recognized the ink stamped across the front of it. Karisha. I counted the envelopes, and it had to be at least twenty-five letters there.

"Momma, I'm sorry.... I," I started to say, but she cut me off.

"Oh, it gets better. here, this is one that came for ME."

I looked at her confused, and she handed me the envelope. I sat down in the chair closest to me and opened the envelope to retrieve the letter. I unfolded the letter and started reading it. I couldn't believe my eyes.

"When I get out, I will catch your son, and you and him will wish I never existed...."

I looked up at my mom who still had the stank look on her face.

"What you do to that girl, Stanley?! And don't you lie to me!"

She sat down across from me.

"Mom, I ain't did shit. This the bitch, I mean, girl, that shot Lala."

My mom looked at me as if she knew I was leaving something out.

"Mom, I swear, I ain't did nothing. She been in jail for like a month and some change now. I haven't talked to her."

"But you talked to her before she went in right? You are just like your father, Stanley. Nothing good is gonna come from you keeping in touch with this girl. Karma is a bitch, baby, and I think you just met yours."

She got up from the table and walked back in the kitchen. I sat at the table a little longer and looked at the letters. Karisha was really a nut case, and now since I blocked her, she was harassing my mom. This shit had to stop.

"Mom, I'm about to go talk to X," I said as I walked out of the house.

When I walked out of the house, I saw a female leaving Xavier's garage. I didn't recognize her until I got closer. It was Lala. She looked different, thicker of course, but her hair was gone. Lala had a long weave the last time I saw her, and now she rocked a fade.

"Aye, lemme holla at you for a minute," I said as I walked up behind her.

She didn't even see me coming. I scared the hell out of her. When she turned around and saw it was me talking to her, her nostrils flared, and she turned back around. I walked up faster and grabbed her arm. She snatched it away from me.

"Don't fucking touch me," she spat as she stood in the middle of the street.

"Lala, you okay?" LaShae called from across the street.

"Yea, I'm good," she said as she finished crossing the street.

I stood in the middle of the street looking stupid and feeling enraged. I walked into the garage, dapped Baby Rag and the other homies. I motioned my head to say, "What's up?" to Xavier as he worked on a cut. I watched him cut dude's hair, but he didn't even look at me. I kept trying to catch his attention while I played like I was paying attention to the other conversations going on.

"Yo', X, lemme holla at you outside right quick."

I got up and made my way to the backyard. I could have sworn I heard X suck his teeth before he turned off the clippers and told dude he'd be right back. Exiting the house, X lit up his doob and took a hit.

"What's up, cuz," he asked me as he ashed it.

"Yo' man, who that you put on Instagram yesterday?"

I got straight to it; I ain't have time to go around the topic at hand.

I laughed as I asked, "Why, my nigga?"

The look I gave him let him know it wasn't a laughing matter. He had to know I knew who it was.

"You know why I wanna know. So who was it?" I asked him one more time.

I felt myself getting angry again.

"My nigga, I'm grown. I ain't gotta explain shit to you," he said as he walked back to the garage door.

"You do gotta explain if you fucking my old bitch," I stopped him in his tracks.

That got everybody's attention in the garage. Baby Rag's head shot up from the conversation he was having.

Xavier

Bitch?

"Aye, watch yo' mouth, my nigga. Matter of fact, get the fuck off my property!" I said to Stanley as he stood in my backyard.

King Scandalous himself had the audacity to question me about fucking his old "bitch?" He had me fucked up as soon as he referred to Lala as a bitch. I didn't care if I was supposed to be keeping shit low key at that point. No way was he about to disrespect the mother of my child.

"I ain't going nowhere until you....or her, answer my question...Matter of fact, I'll go ask her," Stanley said as he turned to walk out of my gate.

I followed behind him.

"Stan, my nigga. You being real extra right now," I said, but he didn't listen. He just kept walking.

He crossed the street and went through the gate. Before he got to the door, I made one last attempt to stop him from getting his own heart broken.

"Cuz, knock it off! Go home, shit! Every time you come over here, it's some shit now!"

I guess I was too loud because before Stanley could knock, Lala and LaShae were standing in the doorway.

Lala

"You like it?" I asked LaShae as I brushed my newly cut hair in the mirror.

"Yes, it fits you, girl," LaShae smiled at my reflection.

"I know, man. A new beginning and a fresh start," I cheesed as I thought about the plans X, and I had been making.

LaShae held Kamille in her arms.

"You like Mommy's hair, baby?" I asked as she stared at me with her big pretty eyes. She cracked a smile. "Oh my gosh! You smiled for mommy!"

Kamille's first smile brought tears to my eyes. The sentimental moment was ruined when we heard men arguing outside. LaShae and I made our way to the front door just in time to see Stanley headed over with Xavier walking behind him. My heart began beating really fast. I thought it was going to beat out of my chest. LaShae opened the door and walked outside. I snail0walked behind her.

"Yo' La, lemme holla at you real quick!" Stanley looked like a bull the way his nostrils flared.

"We ain't got shit to talk about," I said as I stepped in front of LaShae and Kamille.

Xavier chimed in right after, "Yea, my nigga. She said she don't got shit to say to you, so let it go, cuz."

"Cuz? Who the fuck is you? Captain Save-a-slut?" Stanley spat at Xavier.

"Who the fuck you calling a slut?!" I yelled at Stanley.

"Lala, calm down. You just had a baby. C'mon, calm down," LaShae said as she tried to pull me back in the house.

"No, I'm tired of his ass. Don't sit around here and act like you just the most innocent nigga in the situation because you ain't! I don't owe you shit, ESPECIALLY not a conversation!" I yelled and turned back around to walk in the house.

"So you fucking X?"

Stanley's words stopped me in my tracks. My mouth fell open and so did LaShae's. He looked at me with pain and embarrassment in his eyes.

"You been fucking my best friend, Lala? My best friend!"

He walked closer to me, but LaShae stepped in front of me.

"Man, bitch, what the fuck is you gon' do with a ba-…. Wait a fucking minute!" Stanley stopped talking long enough to look at Kamille in LaShae's arms and back at Xavier.

"Quincy!!!!!!!!!!!!!" LaShae yelled out.

"Momma!!!!!!!!!!"

Stanley

The resemblance was undeniable, to say the least. Kamille was chocolate, and that was the only thing that she didn't have of Xavier. My heart hurt. I ain't never felt the pain I felt looking at my best friend and my ex-girlfriend. Snapping me out of my thoughts, my phone vibrated. The screen read "Averie." I answered it with the intention to tell her to call me back later, but when I answered, I heard the pain in her voice.

"Where are you?" She asked me.

"I'm at my mom's house. Wassup?" I replied.

"I need to talk to you. I'm about to pull up. Give me five minutes." Then she hung up the phone.

By now, Lala's mom and Quincy were in the front yard with us, waiting for me to do something stupid.

"So y'all don't have nothing to say?"

I looked from Lala to X, and neither one of them had anything to say.

"Aye Stan, man, just let it go and go home," Quincy insisted.

Quincy was a cool nigga. He wasn't from the hood, but he was cool people.

"Nah, I want answers, and these two muthafuckas gone give 'em to me!" I said.

"Watch your mouth, Stanley," Lala reminded me that I was in the presence of an elder.

"I'm sorry, ma'am," I apologized.

Before I could say anything else, Averie pulled up in front of Xavier's house and hopped out the car.

"What's going on?" she asked as she walked up to me. She looked at everyone standing outside, but her stare landed on Lala. "Is that who I think it is?" She whispered.

"Excuse me?" Lala asked, and LaShae handed Kamille to her husband.

"Here, hold Kamille."

Averie

When I pulled up, I saw Stanley standing the front yard of someone's house. It was actually a small crowd developing. I walked up to him and asked him what was going on and then I saw her. I had never seen her before. I had only heard things about her. She didn't look how I thought she would. The bitch didn't have no hair. I assumed the girl standing near her was her sister or something because the older lady had to be her mother. Her sister handed the baby she was holding to a man when I asked Stanley if she was who I thought she was. That's when I caught sight of the baby.

"Yea, that's Lala," Stanley assured me.

My body started shaking soon after he said that.

"What's wrong with you? Why you shaking?" he asked and looked down at me.

"Why you wanna know who I am?" Lala finally decided to speak up.

I didn't like her tone, or the fact that she spoke to me period.

"Because someone I love took their life because you couldn't be honest about who your child's father is."

She looked at me like she'd seen a ghost. Stanley looked at her then back at me.

"Wait, what?" He asked.

"When I went to pay my condolences, Tony's mom gave me the letter that he wrote me."

"Tony? How you know Tony?" Lala asked curiously.

I turned my attention back to her. "He was my ex-boyfriend before he took his fucking life!"

I could tell that Lala hadn't found out that Tony was dead. She grabbed her chest and squatted on the concrete. Xavier walked up to her to console her. Seeing their embrace made Stanley mad as hell.

"Wait, what the fuck you mean he took his life because she didn't know who the father of her child was? He was the father of her child..." Stanley looked up as if he had just got the missing clue. "You sneaky bitch!"

Stanley ran towards Lala, but Xavier blocked her from his grasp.

"My nigga, I'm not gone tell you again to back the fuck up!" Xavier was losing his patience.

"So, you telling me that Tony killed himself because he found out he wasn't the father of Kamille?" Stanley repeated.

He looked at me for clarification, and I nodded my head. "So La, who is Kamille's dad if it ain't me or Tony?"

Everybody in the front yard looked at Lala and waited for her answer.

Lala

All eyes on me, once again. I told myself I was done lying about the situation and whatever happens will happen. Xavier was still blocking me from Stanley, but nothing could protect me from his murderous glare.

"Xavier is Kamille's dad."

I heard my mom gasp.

"What the hell?" I heard her whisper.

I felt like a million pounds was lifted off of my shoulders. I didn't have the balls to look at Stanley, but when I did look up for a brief second, his eyes were locked on me. I knew he was more hurt than mad. Xavier held me in his arms as we stood there, with his chest poked out.

"Really my nigga? My best friend? My best-fucking-friend, LaTanya?" Stanley asked me.

"It wasn't intentional. I didn't just say, 'Okay, Imma fuck X and get pregnant.' You was out of town doing your shit, and I was left here, alone, just me and your bitches." I said to Stanley as I battled tears. "I didn't do it to spite you. No matter what you think, it wasn't planned."

Stanley stood there looking crazy, and his girlfriend tried to grab his arm. "C'mon babe, let's go."

She tried to pull him away.

"Nah, fuck that! X, for real, cuz? Thirty years of friendship and this is what you do?"

Stanley started walking towards X and me. Xavier pushed me out of the way before Stanley had the chance to swing. He caught X with a right hook, but it didn't seem to faze him. I got off the concrete where I fell and tried to break up the two of them and ended up getting socked in the head. Everything faded to black as I hit the concrete again.

Stanley

"My baby!!!" Lala's mom yelled as she knelt down on the concrete to pick up her daughter.

I didn't mean to hit her, this time. X and I stopped fighting long enough for us to realize she wasn't moving.

"Call 911!!!!!!!" LaShae screamed.

Xavier bent down and held her head in hands. I swear I saw a tear drop out that nigga's eye.

"If she dies, I promise on my life, I will kill you," Xavier said as he held Lala.

Averie grabbed me. "Come on let's go now!" she said as she pulled me towards her car. I got in on the passenger side and sunk into the seat.

"Stanley, what was that about?" she asked.

"What the fuck you think it was about?" I spat at her, irritated by her obvious question.

"You were trying to fight your friend before I pulled up. Why?"

"Because the nigga been fucking my ex-bitch, and thanks to you, I just found out Kamille is his baby. My best fucking friend! I can't believe that bitch, man!" I said as I fished around for my phone in my pocket.

"This is too much," she said as she drove.

"Man, take me back to my car. I don't feel like joining your pity party right now."

She looked at me like I'd lost my mind. She made a U-turn and dropped me off where she picked me up at. Without saying bye, she sped off as soon as I closed the door.

The ambulances were there now. I walked over to my mom's yard and looked on like everyone else.

"Stanley, what happened?" my mom asked coming out of the house with the phone up to her ear.

"I don't know. I just pulled back up, ma," I lied to her as we looked on.

"Oh my gosh! Is that Lala on the gurney?" She looked at me for an answer.

"I don't know, ma. I'm standing where you standing," I replied as I made my way in the house.

Seeing Lala on the gurney brought back feelings from the 4th of July. Yet again, I was the reason why she was in a shitty situation. I was in the house watching television when I heard commotion outside. It sounded like females arguing. I got up and rushed toward the front door to see LaShae and her mom in my yard, arguing with my mom.

"Your abusive ass son hit my sister and knocked her out!" LaShae yelled at my momma.

"Bitch, if you don't get out my momma face, Imma give you what I gave your rat ass sister!" I yelled back as I walked through the door.

My mother turned to me. "Stanley, you told me you didn't know what happened."

She was furious as she looked at me for an answer.

"Ma, I didn't mean to hit Lala. I was swinging at Xavier, and I hit her by accident."

"You was swinging at Xavier? Why?" She asked.

"Yea Stanley, tell her why!" LaShae instigated.

"Because he been fucking Lala, and that's who got her pregnant."

My mom held her chest when I told her that part.

"You got one more time to ever touch my sister, and I promise, I will kill you myself! Stay the fuck away from her!" LaShae spat before she walked back to the house.

She and her mom hopped in the car and drove off. I assumed they were headed towards the hospital.

"Stanley, what is wrong with you!?" my mom yelled at me once we got back in the house. "You are really your father's child, you know that? You walking around here putting your hands on females? Why?!"

She was in my face now. I didn't know what to say; there was really nothing I could say.

"Ma, I'm sorry, I just... I just was mad. I didn't mean to hit her, I swear." I replied.

"You need to leave that girl alone. Yea, she lied to you, but Stanley, you have caused nothing but heartache in her life since the day you two started dating. She got shot behind you on the 4th, got in a fight with your other girlfriend at her baby shower, and now she's headed back the hospital. Let it go, son."

I knew she was right; she was always right. I sat down in the chair nearest to me.

"It just ain't right, ma! Xavier fu-...did it to her and got her pregnant. That's supposed to be my best friend!"

I know I sounded like a little bitch, but I didn't care no more. Shit was hitting home, and it hurt.

"Baby, I get that, but still, you had no right to even approach her about it. You cheated so much. Besides, you have a new girlfriend. Let that girl live her life. You and Xavier are better than that to let a girl come between y'all. Cool off and go talk to him," she said as she rubbed my face. "You gotta let go and let God, baby. You inheriting too much bad karma."

I stood up from the table to give my mom a hug and kiss before I headed out.

"I'll see you later, ma."

I kissed her soft brown cheek. She hugged my neck and gave me a kiss on my cheek.

"Okay. Be safe, son. I love you. I'll always be here for you when you feel like you don't have anyone else; me and Shi'ann," she assured me.

"I know, ma. I know. Love you. "I checked my pockets for my keys and walked towards the front door. Locking it behind me, I hit the alarm, and the lights inside my car came on. When I got to the driver's side, I noticed X pulling out of his mom driveway. He drove in my direction and turned on his headlights. I stared at him as he passed. "Bitch ass nigga!" I said aloud, but I doubt he heard me.

I stopped at Nate's before I headed home. "Gimme that bottle of Patron," I told the dude behind the counter.

"Which one?" he asked.

"Nigga, do it look like Imma buy the small bottle? Gimme that big bottle, cuh."

Irritated with the dumb question, I threw a fifty on the counter. "Keep the change," I said as I walked out the store.

Pushing the start button on my ride, I pulled out my cell and scrolled through my contacts. Stopping at "Crystal," my dick instantly got hard. The way she sucked my dick not too long ago still had my head spending. No matter how long we went without talking, when I called, she came... literally. I pressed her number until the call connected.

"Hello?" she sounded like she was asleep.

"What's up? What you got goin'?" I asked while opening the Patron bottle.

"Shit, laying here. What's up?" she asked.

I knew she was lying. She always said that when I woke her up out of her sleep for some pussy. She enjoyed being my on-call piece of ass. I put the bottle up to my mouth and took a big gulp to the head. "Aaahhhhhhhhhh shiiiit," I said as the nasty taste hit every taste bud on my tongue. Patron was nasty as hell, but it got the job done. "Aye, I'm finna pull up," I said, putting my car in drive.

I hung up the phone before she responded.

Crystal lived off LaBrea and Jefferson, so coming from Compton was a nice little ride. I didn't mind, though. I had my drank and my music to help me forget about all the bullshit that happened tonight. As I sped on the freeway, I took another big gulp of liquor to the face. This time I wasn't paying attention, and I swerved in the lane beside me. The driver honked his horn and yelled something out the window, but I laughed at him. I turned up Jeezy new track featuring Jay-Z, "Seen It All," and bobbed my head to the beat. I sat back in my seat, and my mind was taken over by thoughts of Lala.

Scandalous bitch, I thought to myself.

She had never shown me any signs of disloyalty until now. She really had me believing I was the one that was in the wrong. I shook my head at the thought. My exit was coming up, so I turned on my blinker to get over and hopped in the lane next to me.

There were bright lights and horns as my car slid across the lanes on the freeway. I tried to regain control, but I couldn't grab the steering wheel. My eyesight was beyond blurry. "BOOM!" was the last thing I heard, and everything went black.

Averie

I sped down the streets of Compton; vision was blurred because of the tears I'd been crying since I left Stanley. His bitter, inconsiderate attitude caught me off-guard, like we both didn't just find out terrible news. When I made it in my apartment, I fell out on the couch and cried into my pillows. My heart was breaking more and more. Tony was gone. Terri was having Tony's baby. And Stanley wasn't the man I thought he was. He can say he didn't try to hit Lala, but I saw that he was aiming directly for her. The look in his eyes was the same look he had when he fucked me earlier this morning. He looked possessed. All I wanted was for the thoughts to get out of my head. I wanted to stop thinking about everything. I got up from the couch and went into my bathroom. Before opening the medicine cabinet, I looked at myself in the mirror. My hair was all over my head now, and my eyes were puffy from all the crying I'd done all day.

Retrieving my pills out of the medicine cabinet, I filled the cup that sat on my sink with water and swallowed two Motrin 800s. My head was throbbing. I walked in the kitchen, got a slice of bread, and walked back over to the couch. I closed my eyes and tilted my head back as I chewed the last piece of bread. The tears began to fall over again. Before I

knew it, I was dosing off.

Xavier

I paced the halls at the hospital as Lala was being worked on. LaShae and Quincy were seated near me, and Lala's mom had decided to take Kamille home. It had been a little over two hours since they took her in, and I couldn't help but think the worst. I was going crazy just thinking about everything she'd been going through lately. All the stress on her body. Saying a silent prayer, I was relieved when the doctor came out to talk to us.

"The family of LaTanya?" He looked around.

LaShae stood up and walked over to him first. "I'm her sister. Is she okay?"

She had tears in her eyes, and I could tell she was hoping for the best news.

"LaTanya is in a medically-induced coma. The hit she took to her head caused her to have quite a few seizures since she's been in the back. She will be okay, but of course, we have to put her in observation for a few days."

We all breathed a sigh of relief.

"When can we see her?" LaShae asked.

"You can go sit with her for a few minutes. She's not responsive and please try not to excite her. I'll send my nurse out to escort you guys to her room," the doctor said and walked away from us.

"Whew, man. Lala sho know how to scare us, huh?" I asked jokingly.

Quincy chuckled, "Yea, that girl." He shook his head.

"Thank you for being there for my sister, X. I really appreciate it. I know..."

I cut her off, "I love Lala. I been in love with her for a long time, and that ain't never changing."

LaShae looked up at me with tears in her eyes, "Awwww. Give me a huggggggg!"

We all started laughing.

The nurse came out to escort us to Lala's room. Seeing her in that bed made me sick to my stomach. She didn't deserve it. I walked up to the bed once LaShae and Quincy kissed her cheek and stepped out of the room. I was afraid to touch her as I pulled a chair up to the bed. Grabbing her hand, I brought it to my mouth and kissed it softly. The sounds of her monitors caught my attention. From what I could understand, her heartbeat sped up. I laughed to myself.

"Lala, calm down, I'm here. It's me, X." Again, her monitor sounded off. "Okay Lala, now you being funny," I laughed. I let go of her hand, and the sounds got louder. I grabbed her hand again. "I'm still here, Lala, you gotta chill. I can't stay here long tonight, but I'll be back first thing in the morning and the morning after that. I'll be here when they wake you up."

Hoping that would make her feel a little bit better, I kissed her cheek and walked out of the room. I rode home with Quincy and LaShae because I didn't drive my own car up there. Once I got on the block, my mom was at the door ready with the questions. I walked in the house, and she was waiting for me on the couch.

"So what happened, son?"

I grabbed my head.

"Ma... Lala's baby is my baby. Stanley found out; he tried to fight me and ended up knocking Lala out," I said and finally let the tears fall.

I had been holding in those tears for a while now. My mom rubbed my hand.

"I knew that was your baby the minute her mom showed me a picture. Y'all thought y'all was so slick, but I see and know everything that goes on in this house. I thought you knew that by now," she said with a smirk on her face.

I blushed. "Still can't get nothing past you, huh?"

"Never will, baby....I would like to meet my granddaughter soon."

I stood to leave, and she said, "Be safe out there, baby," and then gave me a hug.

By the time I made it home, it was damn near 11 pm. When I pulled up to my house, the street was pretty empty, so I parked on the street. I walked in and was greeted by silence, something I've grown to appreciate lately. I sat on the couch and pulled out a doob I rolled up earlier. I reached in my pocket for my lighter and turned on the TV with my free hand. I lit the doob as I watched the news. There was a breaking news story; a bad accident happened on the 91 West. I turned up the volume because the wreck took place close to the city. When the camera zoomed in on the car, my body went numb.

"Yes, Jane, it is said that the driver was drunk and crashed into the wall on the 91West near the Harbor Freeway on ramp. It is said that the driver did perish in the crash, although a name has not been released just yet."

Averie

I fell asleep with my head in my pillows on the couch. Tony met me in my dreams again, and this time he spoke to me. He was trying to tell me to go away and don't look back. I reached over to the coffee table to retrieve my cell phone. I had ten missed calls from Stanley's mom's house. I figured it was Stanley calling me from her house phone, so I didn't bother returning the phone call. I didn't realize I'd been holding my pee until my leg started trembling. I looked at my cellphone; it was 11:30. I knew nothing but the news was on, but I needed some type of entertainment.

Tired of being stuck in my own thoughts, I turned my attention to the breaking news story that was on the television. My heart sank into the pit of my stomach when I realized I was looking at Stanley's Benz mangled on the freeway. I blinked twice to make sure I wasn't tripping, but once I opened them and saw the photo of Stan on the TV, I blacked out.

"The victim, identified as Stanley Williams, was rushed to the hospital where he was pronounced dead."

I'm sure God could hear my cries.

I couldn't breathe. I couldn't move. I didn't want to know it was true. How could this happen? Why am I being punished? What did I do to deserve this karma? I shook violently as I sat on my couch. My phone began ringing. I looked at the screen and "Mimi" scrolled across the screen. I rejected the call and sent her straight to voicemail because I didn't feel like talking. I could barely think straight. My phone lit up again, and I answered it this time.

"He....hello?" I sniffled as I talked.

"Are you okay? I just saw the news," Mimi said in a worried tone.

"Noooooooooooooooo," I broke down on the phone.

"I'm on my way, Averie."

She hung up, and I dropped my phone.

Xavier

I've been sitting in the same spot I was in the night before when I see my nigga picture pop up on the TV. I was in disbelief. Yea, we beefed, but that was my best friend all my life. I really didn't want to believe he was gone. My phone interrupted my thoughts. It was my mom.

"Yea," I answered dryly.

"Baby, are you okay?" My mother knew me better than anyone in this world so she knew I was going to try to hide my feelings about this situation.

"Yea, I'm okay, ma. How are you?" I asked in a nonchalant tone.

"I'm okay. Would you come over, please? Stanley's mom is asking for you."

She caught me off guard with that. "Ma, I don't really want to go over there. It's too soon."

"Xavier, get over here now! Everyone is hurting, but they all looking for you!"

She wasn't playing with me. "I'm on my way."

I hung up the phone and put my head in my hands. The tears finally started falling.

My best friend was gone.

As I got dressed, I thought about all the good times Stanley, and I had growing up together. I didn't have any brothers, just a sister. Stanley had all sisters, so we were each other's brothers. It worked out perfectly too. I was the shy guy, and Stanley was always the outspoken one. I chuckled as I thought about this one time we were at the park. We had to have been, like, ten. These older niggas from Nutty Block tried to punk me for my bike. I was small for my age, but Stanley wasn't. Stanley stood up to the big niggas and even fought them for me. It was, like, two of them against a ten-year-old. Stanley held his own though and escaped the fight with just a busted lip.

I wanted to just think about all the good times, but I couldn't ignore the bad times we had just gone through. I wish I would've been able to talk to him, man to man, before he was called home, but I didn't. There was a way for us to get things settled, but neither one of us wanted to be the bigger person. We wanted to be the BIG person.

As I drove to the block, a part of me wanted to turn around. I didn't want to face everyone.

Just as I imagined, the street was packed. *Bad news travels fast*, I thought as I pulled into my mom's driveway. I saw a lot of the homies I wouldn't normally see. It's crazy how it takes a death to bring niggas together. There were females galore. I'm sure a few of them were his "girlfriend," but all of them thought they were the only one.

My mom met me at my car door, "You gonna go over there now?" she asked.

"Yes, ma'am," I replied as I stepped out of the car.

"You need me to come with you?" she asked.

I looked back at her as I proceeded across the street. "Nah, ma. I'm good." Then I flashed her a smile.

I was greeted by Baby Rag as I crossed the street. "You good, cuh?", he asked.

I looked at him and then I looked at the crowd around the house. "I guess."

I walked towards the front door. Entering the house bought back so many memories. You could feel the sadness though. Stanley sisters were seated on the sofa around his mom. As soon as his older sister, Pam, saw me, her face went from sad to pissed.

"The fuck you doin' over here?" she spat in my direction. That made everyone look up to see who she was talking to. Pam and I never got along, not since I fucked her and left her hanging YEARS ago. You would think with her being married and having four kids, she would be over it by now, but she wasn't.

"I came to pay my respects," I said as I walked over to her mother.

"Mom, I'm so sorry," I told her as I hugged her.

As soon as I wrapped my arms around her, she broke down. "My baby gon', Xavier! He's gone!" She looked up at me with tears in her eyes. I could no longer hold mine in.

"He's in a better place, you guys," Stanley's other sister, Chastity, chimed in. She was always the optimistic one, even at times like these.

"Yea, Chas is right. He's in a better place. No more pain or anger filling his soul," his mom spoke up.

I looked at her, wondering where she found the strength to come to terms with the fact that her son was gone.

Averie

At Tony's Funeral

Keeping it together has been the hardest thing ever. Losing two men that I had so much love for basically back-to-back had really taken a toll on me. I took a leave of absence from work. I could barely think straight; there was no way I'd be able to work. Mimi had been at my house since she came over to comfort me when Stanley got in that accident. Usually, I would hate for someone to be in my space, but this time, I didn't mind.

"Averie, it's time to get up."

I woke up to Mimi tapping my shoulder. I heard her walk in my room, and I slid further under the covers before she noticed me. I wasn't ready to get up. I wasn't ready to bury Tony. It pained me to think of him being in a box, a damn box. Tony wasn't the best person, but he sure wasn't the worst. Day after day, I tried to prepare myself for this day because I knew it would be one of the hardest days I'd have to endure.

"C'mon, Averie," Mimi pulled the cover from over my head. "Well, at least you wrapped your hair," she chuckled. I snatched the cover back over my head. "Averie, come on. We're going to be late."

I felt the bed rise and then I heard my door close. I closed my eyes and said a silent prayer, "God, please just get me through this. *Please*."

I took a deep breath and pulled the cover from over my head. I sat up against my headboard and noticed there were clothes laid out for me at the foot of my bed. I made a mental note to buy Mimi a big gift to show her how thankful I am for her. Finally throwing my feet off the bed, I stood up and stretched. I walked over to the clothes that sat at the edge of the bed. I picked up the cream color top and put it up to my breast to make sure it would fit. I laughed a little bit when I looked at the tag. Mimi knew I liked wearing my shirts smaller than normal. The high-waisted cream slacks looked like they would fit me perfect. For that little moment in time, I felt okay, but then I thought about what I was about to do.

After I showered, I looked at my reflection in the mirror, and the bags that sat under my eyes looked like they were full of bags. I looked like shit, and that's exactly how I felt. However, there was no way I was going to go to Tony funeral looking how I felt. He would have wanted me to be beautiful. So for that reason alone, I took out my Mac makeup bag and went to work on my face. When Mimi knocked on the door to check on me, she looked surprised when she saw my face.

Dressed in cream as well, she said, "See? This is the Averie Tony knew and loved."

The mere mention of his name made me weak, but I sucked it up and smiled.

"I'm almost ready," I smiled at her and said.

I walked back into my room and got dressed. When I walked out the room, Mimi was already at the door with her purse.

"You ready to do this?" she asked me as she turned the doorknob.

"I really don't have a choice," I said with a faint smile.

The ride to the church was a quiet one. I could tell Mimi didn't know what to say, but I didn't need her to say anything anyway, I just needed her there for support.

The church was packed. I didn't know Tony knew so many people. As we stood outside to let the family go in first, Ms. Bridgette spotted me as she walked passed.

"Averie," she called out to me.

I grabbed Mimi and walked over to where she stood.

"Hi, Ms. Bridgette," I said in a soft voice.

"Hi, baby, I want you to sit with the family. Tony loved you, so we love you."

Her request brought tears to my eyes. Mimi and I jumped in line behind Ms. Bridgette and began making our way into the church. Out the corner of my eye, I saw Terri mad dogging me as I walked past. I guess she was upset that she wasn't what she thought she was.

Tony's home-going was so beautiful. I cried, I laughed, and I even spoke when it was time to say a few words. I don't know how I did it, because I could never speak in public, but it's like something made me go up there and share my story with the church. Breaking down midway through, Mimi grabbed me and walked me to the restroom. After using the restroom, I stood in front of the sink to wash my hands when I saw Terri in the reflection.

"Don't start nothing in here, Terri," I warned her.

She looked at me and laughed, "You really think you're 'it,' huh? You think he really loved you? He didn't. It was all a big lie; he's always loved me."

I looked at her and let out the loudest laugh I've ever laughed. So loud that Mimi bust in the restroom to make sure

I was okay. When she saw me laughing, she could do nothing but laugh too, not even knowing what I was laughing at.

"Terri, I wish you well and congrats on your child."

I walked out of the restroom with my head held high.

Xavier

It's been about a week since Lala has been in this coma. The doctors planned on waking her up today, and I was so happy about that. It was sickening for me to look at her day after day lying in that bed. I really hated seeing her that way. I was still coming to terms with Stanley's death, and once she was awake, I would have to tell Lala what happened to him as well. That might've been the hardest part because no matter how mad Lala was at Stanley, I knew she forgave him and would be devastated about his death. LaShae dropped Kamille off to me at the hospital. She'd been bringing her to see Lala every day. As Kamille and I sat and waited for Lala to wake up, I could only think about how much Lala and Kamille had been through. I know Kamille probably won't remember any of it, but Lala would.

I was walking back into the room with Kamille when I heard Lala's voice. It was raspy, but it was her.

"Where's my baby?"

She tried to focus her eyes on me, but I knew she probably couldn't see very well.

"Well, hello to you too," I said as I smiled at her.

She tried to smile back, but she couldn't. When she noticed Kamille in my arms, she tried to lift herself up. Immediately she wrenched in pain.

"Lala, you can't be doing all that moving," I said as I walked over to her and laid Kamille on her chest.

A single tear escaped her eye.

"I missed her," she said as she looked down at Kamille.

"She missed you too," I replied as I looked at the two of them.

"So what happened to me?" she asked curiously. I didn't know how to answer the question. "I know Stanley hit me, Xavier," she surprised me.

The doctors said she might not remember anything that happened recently, but I probably should have known that wasn't the case when she recognized Kamille. I still didn't know how to tell her everything else that went down that night. I sat down in the chair across from her and took a deep breath.

"What's wrong?" she asked me with worry written all over her face.

"Lala, I need to promise me that you're going to stay calm, okay?" I told her before I began telling her the story.

"Okay," she closed her eyes and took a deep breath.

"La, Stan died." Almost on cue, her monitors went haywire. "Lala, you have to calm down," I said and got up and walked over to console her.

Lala

Maybe I didn't hear him correctly. I mean, my monitors were kind of loud.

"What did you say?" I asked while trying to catch my breath.

I was hoping Xavier didn't say what I thought he said. If what I thought to be said was right, X said that Stanley was dead.

"Stanley got in a real bad car accident and died, Lala."

Xavier gave me the saddest puppy dog eyes. *First Tony and now Stanley,* I thought to myself. The tears started pouring out of nowhere.

"I....I....I don't know what to say," I said as I trembled.

A nurse came rushing into the room.

"GET OUT! I'M OKAY! GET THE FUCK OUT!"

The poor girl looked like she was going to piss herself. She immediately exited the room.

"Lala, baby, please calm down," Xavier said.

I looked at him like he was shit.

"Promise me you had nothing to do with it," I said.

The look on his face let me know that I'd gone too far. I didn't mean to accuse him of anything, but that's the first thing that came to my mind.

"You think I would kill my best friend? I don't care what the fuck me and Stan ever went through; it ain't never got that deep, and it fasho didn't get that deep this time!"

He looked me up and down like I wasn't shit.

"Xavier, I didn't mean..." he cut me off.

"You didn't mean what? What else could you possibly mean when you say some shit like that?" He looked at me for an answer I couldn't give him. "You know what? Imma just go. I'll be back to see you tomorrow." Xavier said as he attempted to grab Kamille off the side of me where she was lying.

"Let me kiss her first," I pleaded.

He picked her up and brought her head to my lips. I kissed her and rubbed my finger across her nose.

"Later," he said as he walked out without a hug or kiss.

I didn't mean to offend Xavier. I just had to make sure he didn't have anything to do with Stanley's death. While I was trying to reposition myself in the bed, there was a knock on the door. The nurse that I'd yelled at not too long ago was back.

"I'm sorry about that," I said as I wiped my face.

"It's okay, ma'am. I just need to check your vitals."

I obliged. While she checked everything, I thought about Stanley: all our good times, our bad times, our horrible times. I couldn't believe he was gone. I didn't want to believe he was gone. I thought about Tony, too. *How did I manage to lose two lovers in a matter of weeks*? I thought. I still hadn't come to terms with the fact that Tony took his life because of me. That thought made me sick to my stomach. Never in a million years did I think someone would take their life because of me. I guess that was the karma of it all.

Xavier

A week later

Upon Lala's release, she and Kamille came to stay with me. She needed someone to help her with Kamille and herself. I didn't want nobody else doing what I should be doing, so of course, I opened my home to her. It was the morning of Stanley's funeral, and against my wishes, Lala wanted to attend. I just didn't want her to get too stressed out. I know how much stress she was under, but I also knew that Stanley meant a lot to her, so there was no way she was missing his home going services.

When we arrived at the church, dirty looks were shot in my direction when they saw Lala on my arm. It didn't seem to faze her, though. She kept her head held high and feet moving forward. She wore a black fitted dress, which hugged every single new curve her body developed over the last few weeks. I couldn't help but stare at her as she got dressed that morning. People spoke and gave their condolences to us, but others just stared in disgust. I didn't give a fuck. I never gave a fuck about what someone had to say about what I was doing.

"Let them stare, babe. They don't know our story," Lala said, and she grabbed my hand and squeezed it.

I looked at her and smiled. Her strength and courage never ceased to amaze me.

The service was nice. They sent my boy off the right way. I was surprised when they read my name along with his other siblings. It actually brought a tear to my eye. When it was time for remarks, I walked to the podium. People looked at me crazy, probably wondering what the hell I had to say. I looked over all of them and found Lala in the crowd. She smiled at me, letting me know it was okay.

"First off, I need to give honor to God, for he is the center of my life. A lot of y'all might know me, and some of y'all might not. Stan was my best friend, my brother, actually. He was more than a best friend. We grew up together, we fussed, we fought, and we beat other people up," I paused to laugh. "I wish I would've been able to talk to him before he was called home." I looked at his casket. "You are forever my only brother, cuh. I'm sorry, Stan. I love you, boy."

I walked off back to my seat before I broke down. When I sat down, Lala grabbed my hand and looked at me with assuring eyes.

After the service, the block was lit. There were people everywhere, from all over. Stanley was seriously loved by almost everybody he came in contact with, minus the rival gang members he might've ran into every now and then. I was sitting outside near the porch when Sheila pulled up with Shi'ann.

Shi'ann ran to me squealing, "Uncleeeeeee!"

Sheila yelled, "Get away from him, Shi. C'mon lets go see granny."

She mad-dogged me when she walked past. I shook it off. I expected it from her ignorant ass. I saw Lala coming towards the house. Well, everyone noticed her approaching. I met her halfway because she had Kamille in her hands.

"Wassup," I asked her as we met on the sidewalk.

"Nothing, just coming to see what you're up to..." she said as she looked around and noticed everyone looking at her kind of funny.

"You wanna just go back to your mom's house? I'll come in and chill with you and Kamille until we go home."

She looked at me like I was crazy.

"You think I give a damn about these people? I don't care about nothing they have to say. I know what I did. They think they know the whole story so let them assume. I don't care."

I promise; Lala's strength always surprised me.

Averie

When I walked into the church, I sat in the back, the total opposite of when I went to Tony's funeral. Stanley and I were new to each other, so his family didn't really know of me. I watched all the women pile in the church, and I'd be lying if I said I didn't suspect more than half of them were either ex-girlfriends or side bitches. They just had that look.

I noticed a semi-familiar face sitting close to the family. When she turned her head, her side profile revealed her identity. It was Lala. I expected her to be there, but then again I didn't, because last I'd heard, she was in the hospital in a coma. I guess she pulled through. I cursed God for that. In my eyes, she needed to be lying in the casket, not Stanley. She should've been lying in Tony's casket as well. My hands shook as I thought about putting Tony in the ground because of her dumb ass.

Stanley's so-called "best friend" stood up when it was time for remarks. I couldn't wait to hear what he had to say. Thinking he would get up there and lie, he surprised me and actually told the truth at the altar. The way Lala looked at him once he sat down made me envy her. She still had a man that loved her, even after the other two were dead and gone. *Must be nice,* I thought as I stood up to make my way out of the church. It was a closed-casket service due to the severity of Stan's injuries, and I had to walk past her on my way down the aisle. It took everything in me not to jump on her. I kept my composure, though. Stanley would have wanted me to act like a lady. I stopped at the first pew and gave his mother a kiss on the cheek. On my way out of the church, I looked back, and Lala was staring at me. I rolled my eyes and walked out.

I didn't want to go to repast alone, so I had Mimi come with me. We'd been attached at the hip lately; I liked it, though. When we pulled up, the street was almost too packed to get through, so we had to park on the side street. I didn't mind, though. I didn't want to park too close anyway. We stopped and got chicken and a cake for the family, so we were a little later than everyone else. When we walked up to the house, I noticed a man and lady holding a baby standing on the sidewalk. Something in me just knew it was this Lala bitch. As I got closer, low and behold, I confirmed that it was her, in the flesh. As we approached them, Xavier noticed me and pulled Lala out of the way. She turned around to see why and saw me, her facial expression read, "This bitch," and mine read, "YEP, IT'S ME." I could barely hold it together as we got closer, so I handed Mimi the bag I was holding, just in case she tried something. When she saw me do that, she handed her baby to Xavier. He looked dumbfounded, but quickly caught on and snatched Lala behind him.

"What the fuck!" she yelled.

"Don't come over here starting no shit," Xavier said to me as I approached the two of them.

"Nigga, please, I ain't gotta start shit. I just want to finish something," I said as I looked at Lala, who stood behind him, ready for whatever.

"You got something you want to say to me?" Lala asked as she looked at me up and down.

Mimi grabbed me, "Not here, Averie. Not now."

Looking at the child in Xavier's arms, "Fucking bastard baby," I said as I began walking away.

Lala

"Bastard baby," the punk bitch whispered as she walked past Kamille and Xavier.

"What the fuck you just call my daughter?"

At this point, I was livid. I never started shit with anyone, but these bitches keep coming for me. I don't get it. Averie didn't respond. She kept walking towards Stanley's house.

Xavier grabbed me, "Come on. Let's go to my mom's house."

As we crossed the street, I turned around, and Averie was staring at me with daggers in her eyes.

"BITCH, DO YOU HAVE A PROBLEM?" I yelled across the street at her.

Xavier grabbed me again, "La, come on, cuh. Stop! I'm tired of all the drama!" he said through clenched teeth.

"Yea, listen to your baby daddy," the bitch said.

When she said "baby daddy," she made air quotes with her fingers. Before Xavier could grab me again, I ran across the street. Averie thought she was hard, but she wasn't quick enough for me. I tried to bash her fucking face in with my fist and the rings I wore. Her friend tried to jump in, but Baby Rag was standing close enough to run over and grab her.

"Nah, bitch. We catch fair ones over here," I heard him say to her.

Averie didn't stand a chance against me and my new weight. I wrapped her hair around my hand and pounded at her face with my free hand.

"You watch your mouth when you're talking to my baby!" With each word, I landed a punch.

She tried to wiggle out of my grip, but she couldn't. My body weight on top of her was too much. Before I could land any more punches to her fast, I felt someone grab me and pick me up in the air.

Arms flailing and legs kicking, Xavier managed to get me off the bitch. As her friend tried to help her up, she decided to talk some more shit.

"You hoe ass bitch! Fucked all of Compton and didn't know who yo' baby daddy was!!"

"You still talking, bitch?!!!!!!"

I tried to get out of Xavier's tight grip, but I couldn't.

"X, let me fucking go!!" I demanded.

He refused. By this time a crowd formed, and LaShae came sprinting out of the house. She looked lost, but once she caught sight of Averie still yelling obscenities on the sidewalk, she ran up on her. Nobody saw LaShae coming except X and I. Before he could holler out to Baby Rag to grab her, she had Averie against the gate, fucking her up some more. Baby Rag finally was able to grab LaShae and dragged her back in my mom's house. Xavier wouldn't let me go back across the street until they put Averie in the car. Once she was in the car and being driven away, he let me go, and I walked across the street back to my mom's house. Everybody was looking at me; some were whispering. I still held my head high and didn't give a fuck because none of them knew the real.

Once inside the house, LaShae was in the den still going off. Baby Rag sat on the couch and looked at her pace back and forth.

"These bitches gone learn to stop messing with my little sister! Just let her fucking live," she broke down.

I never knew all my poor decisions were causing the people around me so much pain and agony.

"It's ok, sis. I'm okay," I said as I walked into the den.

"I know you're okay, but damn, this shit is tiring, La. When will it end?"

I couldn't even answer the question for her.

Averie

The car ride home was silent. I used the napkin Mimi handed me to wipe the blood off my face. I was horrified when I looked in the mirror. Lala really got me good.

"You know, I know some people..." Mimi started as she gave me a devilish look.

I already knew what she meant, and normally I would want no parts of it, but this shit just got personal.

"Bitches gon' learn," I said as I sat back in my seat.

Karisha

Two months later

Seeing Stanley's picture plastered on the TV a few months ago made me sick to my stomach. I don't know if I was mad that he died or mad that I didn't get to kill him. I've been in here for almost two months, and I still remember the day Stanley told me not to call his phone anymore. None of that mattered right now though. As I looked at the TV screen in the REC room, I almost lost my balance. I remembered this story airing a few months ago, but I never got to see who the person was. This couldn't be true. I held my stomach. I thought about my unborn child. I thought about my baby growing up without a mother or a father. Before I could make it to a trashcan, I gagged and threw up on the table I sat at.

"Ugh, bitch! You gone clean that shit, too," said one of the dykes I couldn't stand.

I flipped her off and made my way back to my cell. Once inside my cell, I let all the tears fall. My heart was definitely broken now. My heart broke for my child and myself; we had nobody anymore.

There was no way I was going to allow my child to grow up in the same foster system that I did. Stanley was supposed to be its way out of that lifestyle before it even got here. I had to find a way to ensure that my baby would have a chance in this world. That's when it hit me: I would write his mother a letter, apologize for my last letter, and let her know Stanley had a baby on the way. That seemed like the only thing I could do right now, considering my family was no longer speaking to me.

I really had mixed emotions because he did me wrong, but now that he was gone, I felt broken in this piece of shit. No friends, no family. I didn't know what to do until one day I was called for a visit. I sat anxiously at the table waiting to see who was going to walk through the door. Every visiting day I wished it was Stanley who came to see me, but after seeing the news, I knew that was never going to happen. Baby Rag came walking in with the biggest smile on his face. Baby Rag and I had messed around a few times while I was messing with Stanley. I needed eyes where I wasn't able to be, so I did what I had to do.

I almost puked when I looked up to see him approaching my table. I mustered up the biggest smile I could as he approached my table. He came bearing snacks and shit.

"Hey, bae," I stood and hugged him.

Thank God they watched us as closely as they did. Sometimes I would hug Rag, and his dick would be hard as fuck. If he got the chance, I knew he would try to fuck me right there in the visiting room.

"Wassup, ma," he said as he sat down across from me. "You looking kinda chunky," he snickered. "You been eating in here, huh?"

I didn't laugh at his comment, nor did I tell him I was expecting. I just smiled at him.

"So what made you come see me?" I asked him.

He looked kind of hurt when I asked that, and I felt bad because he had always been nice to me.

"I just came to check on you, cuh, you know, since... since Stan died. I figured you were going through it, considering y'all had a thing going on," he explained.

That was sweet of him to check on me, I thought to myself.

"Yes, I saw it on the news. Shit crazy. How's everyone taking it?" I asked.

"I mean, shit ... His family taking it pretty hard. The hood taking it hard," he said. He knew what I really wanted to know. "Lala, she good, man. She took it pretty hard. Shit went down, though, leading up to his death, so I don't know how she really feeling," he explained.

"Shit? What kind of shit?" I was all ears now.

Baby Rag had word vomit. "Yea man, we all found out that Xavier is Lala's baby daddy, not Stanley or her ex-nigga. I can't remember cuh name."

My jaw flew open. I couldn't believe what I'd just heard.

"Damn, for real?" I asked Baby Rag.

He smiled at me and said, "Yea man, shit got real, real deep. Lala and Stanley's girlfriend got in a fight at the repast."

I felt my stomach turn.

"His girlfriend?" I raised my eyebrow.

"Yea, his girlfriend. Some chick named Averie."

I made a mental note of her name.

"Damn, that's crazy," I said as I silently cried to myself.

"Other than that, you ain't missing shit. Aye man, you really gained some weight," he looked at me over the table.

I put my arm in front of my stomach so he couldn't see the little bulge I did have, but it was too late.

"You pregnant, cuh?" he asked.

"No," I replied as I looked away.

"Karisha, I've been to jails to visit bitches. I know my shit. That wristband means you're pregnant," he pointed out the red wristband I wore on my right wrist.

I looked down at my wrist then up at him.

"Who the baby daddy?"

He eyed me suspiciously. I felt like his eyes were burning through me.

"Stanley," I said with my head down.

I didn't want to look up at him. I could only imagine the hurt in his eyes. Baby Rag, on several occasions, had asked me to have his baby, and I said hell no. I made sure we were protected at all times. Except for the last time we fucked; he didn't use protection, nor did he pull out. When the doctor told me I was pregnant in the hospital, I automatically thought about Baby Rag because he was my most recent fuck.

"You sure, cuh?" he asked me in a deep baritone.

It took me a few seconds to answer him, and when I opened my mouth to say something, he cut me off. "You want it to be cuh baby so bad, you know that's my fucking baby."

He was mad now.

"Rag... I ... I don't know," I tried to hold back tears. Pregnancy made me more emotional than ever.

"Nah, you know that's me, that's my seed. Imma let you keep lying to yourself, though. Once you have it, we can get a DNA test. If it ain't mine, then we know whose it is."

He stood up to walk out. He took a few steps away from the table and turned around.

"And just because I'm a stand-up nigga, Imma put money on your books to make sure you feed my... that baby."

He looked disgusted as he walked away from me. I felt numb as a Novocain recipient as I sat and waited for the guard to come back to get me. Baby Rag was right: I did know that it was a better chance of him being my baby daddy than Stanley. Still, a part of me didn't want to let Stanley go at all. Walking back to my cell, I felt depressed. The reality of Stanley really being gone was setting in, and there was nothing I could do about it. I loved that man with every piece of me. Yea, shit was crazy, but it was *ours. We* had that connection and couldn't nobody top that or take that from me. I decided to take my chances and write Stanley one more letter. I knew he was gone, but someone would intercept it and hopefully read it. Sitting down on my cot, I pulled out my notebook and pen and began writing. Once I was done, I sealed it and put a stamp on it. I planned on sending it off the next day.

Averie

6 months later

Life had finally begun to go back to the way it was before the drama. I'd been back at work for a few months now. There hadn't been any run-ins with chicks, and dudes were not even on my mind. I needed time to heal from everything that I'd experienced. After Lala and I fought, I vowed that I would get her back, when she least suspected it. I no longer wanted the help nor have a friendship with Mimi because it turned out she was a snake.

You see, Mimi wasn't playing when she said she knew some people, but it kind of caught me off guard when she told me about the person she knew. Some chick named Karisha; supposedly she and Lala had big beef, but now Karisha was locked up. I didn't understand how she would be any help to me and my plot, but Mimi had it all worked out.

Mimi and Karisha went back from their childhood days. Mimi told me she met Karisha when she was younger. She lived on her block, and all the boys liked her because of her distinctive eye color. Supposedly the bitch had purple eyes. I would have to see that for myself, though. Anyway, Karisha said that she knew Lala and would help us get her. I still didn't understand how they were going to set that up from the inside, until one day when Mimi came over to have drinks with me. It was a little weekend ritual of ours. During our conversation, she slipped up and told me that Karisha use to fuck with Stanley and that she was pregnant in jail. I don't know why Mimi didn't think to tell me all this when she initially told me who Karisha was, but the shit bothered me. I later found out that Mimi too had fucked with Stanley while I was messing with him. A drunk mind unleashes a sober tongue. I beat Mimi ass before I threw her out of my apartment that night.

I was basically alone now; no friends and my family wasn't really around. I had nobody,
but I did have my pride and I was too prideful to let Lala get away with that she'd done to me, Tony and Stanley. Yes, I blamed her for everything, every death, and every bad thing that had happened over that course of time. While being a loner, I'd picked up shooting. I would go to the range by myself at least twice a week. I wasn't a sniper, but I was pretty good for a clean shot. Now that I had the tools, I just needed to put the plan in action.

Lala's time was coming soon.

Lala

My life was finally coming back together. I was back at work. Xavier and I just moved into a new place. Kamille was a happy, bouncy seven-month-old. I couldn't complain about anything at this point.

"X, can you bring me Kamille's clothes?" I yelled from the bathroom where I had just taken Kamille out the bath.

As soon as Xavier came walking in the door, Kamille went nuts.

"Hi, baby," he smiled at her. She cooed at him, which always made his smile brighter.

"C'mon, calm down so I can get you dressed, stinky," I said as I put her on her changing table. Once Kamille was dressed, I tried to get myself dressed. Xavier made that difficult, though; he kept touching me, trying to seduce me.

"NO!" I laughed. "Your family is waiting on us."

He pouted and walked out of the bedroom.

It was the annual Labor Day block party. Just like 4th of July, this was another popping event. I was kind of nervous, considering what had happened on the last 4th of July, but once I saw my family and Xavier's family, I felt safe. There were kids everywhere, running around, having water fights. I looked around, enjoying the view of everyone enjoying themselves. "Gimme my baby," LaShae scared me as she walked up behind me, trying to pry Kamille out my arms. Kamille smiled as soon as she saw her TT. "Bitch, you scared me," I said as I held my chest. "My bad, soulja. I know them nerves bad," LaShae laughed at me. "Yea, whatever. Here, I gotta go find my man." I kissed Kamille and handed her to my sister. I walked down the street towards the basketball courts.

Why is it that men tend to show out when their girlfriends watch them play their sport? I laughed to myself at Xavier as he tried to be LeBron on the court against the youngsters. Baby was tired. I could see it in his face, but because I was watching, he showed out. He made a three-pointer and I cheered for him. "Go baby!" The people around the courts all let out an "Awwwww," being funny of course. When they finished the game, the big homies ended up beating the little homies. "Pay homage, little niggas," Xavier said as he walked past the young boys, headed in my direction. He came in for a kiss. "Ewww! You all sweaty and shit," I play pushed him away. "You like this sweaty shit, girl. Quit playing," he said as he pulled me close and kissed me. "Imma go shower real quick. Thank God I still got clothes over

here, man," he said as we walked back towards his mom
house.

Averie

When I pulled up to the block party, there were so many people around. Everyone was enjoying themselves. I scanned the crowd for Lala bitch ass and couldn't see her, so I decided to get out the car and walk around. If anything, people would think I was a relative of someone on the street. Having checked the bullets in my .22, I put it in my purse and got out the car. The sun was beaming that day as it did every Labor Day. I looked a Plain Jane—white shirt and jean shorts. I didn't want to dress up because I didn't know if I would have to fight this bitch again. As I maneuvered through the street, making sure to stay incognito, I saw the bitch that ran up on me after Lala did. I assumed it was her sister; I remembered her from the day Stanley made Lala hit her head. She looked at me like she knew me, but I lowered my head and kept walking.

Approaching the basketball courts, I ran right into Lala and Xavier. Lala was too into her conversation to notice me, but Xavier noticed me right away. "What the fuck you doing here?" he asked harshly. His nostrils flared, and his jaw tightened. Before Lala could see who he was talking to, I took off on her. I gave her 2 punches to her face, which left her stumbling backward dazed. "Yea, bitch, you don't like when it happens to you, huh?" I yelled. I was hyped, but it didn't last long. I felt something hard crashing against my face, and I swear I heard my jaw click. It was Xavier that he'd punched me in my face. Now I was the one stumbling backward. By this time, Lala had come back to and was on my ass. She grabbed me by my purse strap and socked me as hard as she could in my face. I tried to keep my balance, but I fell. Once I was on the ground, Lala repeatedly kicked me in my face. I couldn't do anything but curl into fetal position and take the kicks. When she was doing kicking and yelling obscenities at me, I reached for my purse, which wasn't too far from me. I pulled out my gun and thought, *Forget aiming*. I just pulled the trigger over and over again, in every direction, in hopes of hitting and killing Lala or her bum baby daddy.

When I opened my eyes, they were still standing, but I heard screaming coming from the direction I'd come from. "The baby!!! Kamillleeeeeeeeeeeeeee!!!!!!!!!!!!!!!!!!!" was all I heard before I blacked out on the concrete. The next time I opened my eyes, I was in the hospital, handcuffed to the bed. I tried to move my arm, but I noticed I couldn't; it was in a sling. My other arm was handcuffed to the bed. "You're just going to hurt yourself more if you keep tryna move," said the nurse that was in the room. "Wh-...how did I get here?" I asked her. "The ambulance brought you here," she replied dryly. "Wha-...why am I handcuffed?" I asked. "Because you're under arrest for the murder of Kamille-Marie," she replied even harsher.

"I did what?" I asked the nurse. I must've heard her wrong. "You really don't know what you did? She looked at me with disgust in her eyes. "You shot a seven-month-old child," she replied as she walked out of the room. When her words finally registered, all I could was cry. But my tears soon stopped when I thought about hurting Lala. I didn't care about killing her baby anymore, as long as she felt the pain that I felt when I buried Tony and Stanley. I wiped my face and got comfortable in the hospital bed, seeing as how this would be my last comfortable resting spot before I was released and arrested.

Lala

My body was numb. I could hear people around me talking, but I couldn't tell you what they were saying. I closed my eyes real tight and said a silent prayer. I prayed that when I opened them, this would all be a nightmare.

Xavier sat to my left with LaShae on my right. In front of me was a young black doctor. Surrounding him was what looked like the whole block plus my family. Everyone held someone. As the doctor explained what happened, they all sighed and shook their heads. Xavier grabbed my hand tighter. LaShae tried to keep a face of stone, but I could see the tears slipping out of her big brown eyes. When the doctor kneeled down in front of me, my hearing came back. "Ma'am, I really did all that I could do. There was just too much damage, and her body was too small to handle the trauma," he held my hand in his and searched my eyes. All I could do was stare at him. I finally managed to open my mouth, "I understand..........thank you so much for all that you did." I then squeezed his hand. "You can see her, to say your last goodbyes," he said to everyone around him. "Parents and immediate family first," the young white nurse came from behind the doctor and spoke to the crowd. LaShae looked at me/ "You sure you can do this right now?" she asked. I nodded my head *yes* and stood up from my seat.

The emotions that I battled were the most intense emotions I've ever felt. I didn't know if I wanted to breakdown, fight, rejoice because my baby wouldn't have to suffer and live with my sins, or just die. Death seemed like the best idea, the more I thought about it. I looked down at Xavier as he still sat in the chair beside mine. His head was lowered. I knew he was crying, and he didn't want anyone else to see it. I tugged his arm to get him to stand, and when he finally did, we both exhaled in unison. "Please follow me," the nurse led us to the room where Kamille laid. When we reached the door, I didn't want to go in. Now I was coming to. My body began to shake, my teeth chattered, and my hands felt like they were dripping sweat. Xavier squeezed my hand tighter, and something about it gave me strength. The room was cold; it smelled like death.

The sight of the white sheet covering the hospital cribbed made me sick to my stomach. *My baby,* I thought, *my chocolate baby was chocolate no more.* Her skin was a color I can't even name. Xavier broke down completely when his eyes fell on her body under the sheet. I tried my best to keep it together and be the strong one, but when I touched Kamille, it was like reality hit. My baby was gone. My baby. The child I carried, the child I breastfed, the child I woke up to and for every day was dead. DEAD.

I rubbed her cheek as my tears fell on her face. Xavier rubbed my back; he couldn't look at Kamille. "Baby, you have to look at her. She's peaceful, babe. No more pain, no more nothing. She's at peace, Xavier," I said to him as I rubbed his back. I felt his chest cave in because he was crying that hard. I don't know when I became the stronger one, but I didn't mind We needed each other. Xavier finally turned to face the baby crib in front of us. He took a deep breath before he opened his eyes. Once his eyes met her body, the tears came back, hard. "She's gone," he repeated a few times as if he was trying to get it through to himself. I bent down to kiss Kamille on her cheek. The coldness broke my heart into pieces. "Mommy will be with you soon," I whispered in her ear before I turned to walk out the door.

Xavier

Lala didn't say much on the way home; I didn't expect her to, though. I couldn't imagine the amount of pain and guilt she was feeling right now. I looked over at her, and she was looking out the window as we drove down the dark streets. "Babe, you feel like eating?" I asked as I drove toward our apartment. She didn't respond. "Lala....are you hungry?" I asked again, and this time I turned down the radio so she could hear me. She looked at me with tears in her eyes. "Did my baby die because of me? Was it my fault?" she cried to me. I didn't know what to say. I knew it was guilt she was feeling, but I didn't know how to comfort her. "Baby, its' not your fault. You didn't pull the trigger," I said. "But it was my fault that bitch pulled the trigger; it's my fault Tony's dead, Stanley's dead, and now my baby. MY fucking baby," she began socking the seats in the car. I pulled over to the side of the road. "Lala, calm down, baby. Just...just calm down." I tried to grab her arms, but she was too quick.

"No! I can't calm down!" she cried hysterically. "My baby is gone! She's dead, X!!! That bitch shot her, and she's never coming back! Kamille was my life! My reason for waking up every morning! I didn't even get to be her mommy!!" she cried harder. I couldn't do anything; I just let her vent. I knew she felt guilty, and I knew why she felt that way. I felt guilty too, though. Had I not been a fake ass best friend, Kamille would've been Stanley's, and he would still be here and so would Kamille. I looked at Lala and wanted to apologize to her so bad, but I knew that nothing I could say would make this any better for her. She fell back into the seat and covered her face with her hands. "Just take me home, please. I want to go home." She didn't need to say anything else. I drove the rest of the way home, trapped in my own thoughts.

When we pulled up to our apartment, I barely had the car in park before Lala jumped out and slammed the door. I knew she was hurting, but I felt like she was being inconsiderate of the fact that I was hurting too. I looked in the rearview mirror like I would do every time I parked. Usually, Kamille was in her car seat in back there, but this time when I looked, the car seat was empty. I didn't see her big eyes that matched mine; I didn't see anything, just the memories of her being back there. Locking the doors, I made my way into the apartment. Lala left the door wide open. I shook my head and reminded myself that she wasn't in her right state of mind. The bathroom light was on, and there was music blasting from being from behind the closed door. Wale played throughout the whole house. I smelled weed burning too. Lala must've decided to take a bath or something and try to relax.

I decided to do the same. Sitting down on the couch, I took my phone out my back pocket. I was on 10%, and it lit up in my hand. Declining the call, I scrolled down to my missed calls. There were a bunch of 'em. My mom called me twenty-five times; I knew she was worried. I clicked the icon to dial her number, and she picked up on the second ring. "Baby...please, please tell me she's okay baby." I could hear the hope in my mom's voice. I didn't want to tell her that her grandbaby, my daughter, died. "Momma....she's...she's gone, momma." As the words sunk in on both sides of the phone, my eyes began pouring tears that I'd managed to hold in. "Noooooooooooooooooooooooooooooooooooooooooooooo, " she cried into the phone. Hearing my mother cry broke my heart even more. I didn't know what to say to mend her broken heart. "Baby...baby, I'm sorry. I'm sooo sooo This time she yelled. sorry. Where's Lala?" At that very moment, I smelled smoke. I took a few sniffs of the air to make sure it wasn't the weed I was smelling. This time it was real smoke. "Hold on, momma."
I put my phone down on the couch and walked towards the hallway where the bathroom was.

My eyes started burning as soon as I hit the corner of the hallway. There were flames coming from under the bathroom door. I panicked. I tried to charge into the door, but there was too much smoke, and it felt like it was filling my lungs. Blinded by the smoke I banged on the bathroom door, "Lala!!!!!!!!!!!!!!" I kicked the door, and it opened. There was so much smoke, "Lala!!! Baby!!!!" I tried to see through the flames, but I couldn't. I tried to feel around the bathtub, but everything was hot. My skin felt like it was burning off, but I refused to leave Lala behind. I wouldn't be able to live with myself if I did. I tried to yell her name again, but the smoke and heat was too much. I felt faint.

"Xavier! Xavier!!!!" My eyes shot open and darted around the room. "Xavier!" I looked over to my left, and Lala had her head raised off her pillow looking at me crazy. "What the hell is wrong with you? You having a nightmare? You started yelling my name in your sleep. Look, you're sweaty as hell. Babe, are you okay," she asked me. I sat up with my back against the headboard, feeling my chest. My beater was soaking wet. I looked at Lala again, "Where's Kamille?" I asked. "She's at your mom house, remember? Her and Tia stayed the night, too excited about the block party." Se looked at me like I was crazy. That's when it started coming back to me. Kamille and Tia stayed the night at my mom house because Tia was excited about the block party, and she wanted Kamille to stay too. It was Kamille's first time spending the night with my mom. She always promised Lala and me a break. "You okay?" Lala was now sitting up against the headboard with me. I grabbed her hand and looked at her, "I had a dream that Averie shot Kamille, and you died in a fire." The look on her face read nothing but fear. "Well," she finally managed to find her words, "I'm still here, Kamille is still here, and we aren't going anywhere." She leaned over and kissed me. I grabbed her face and kissed her back like it was my last time. "Marry me," I said in between kisses. She pulled away from me and looked at me like I had lost my mind. "Whaaat did you say?" she asked. I could hear a little bit of excitement in her voice.

I let go of her hand and reached over to my nightstand. I opened the drawer and pulled out the little black box. When I turned to Lala with it, her eyes looked like they were going to pop out of her head. She covered her face and started crying. "Whaaaa...where did you get that from?" she asked me as I handed her the box. "I've had it since the day you sent me the picture of Kamille after she was born. I knew I wanted to be with you, and I knew we would be together. I didn't care about nothing else. I was ready to go to war with Stanley over you." I thought about Stanley in that instance. "I didn't want him to die, though," I had to assure her. "LaTanya, I love you with all my heart. Tia loves you, my mom loves you, we all love you. I love my daughter. You gave me a life, Lala. I really thank you for that. I know shit ain't been the best, but I know we can grow from all of this."

I grabbed the box out of her hand and opened it, showing her the three-karat chocolate diamond I'd picked out for her. "Will you marry me Lala?" I asked her. Tears came pouring out her eyes, and she waved her hands like she was drying her nails. "Yes, baby! Yes!!!" She hugged my neck and kissed me all over my face.

Epilogue

Karisha spent the rest of her pregnancy incarnated. She delivered a healthy baby boy, whom she named "Lesson Williams" on November 10, 2014. Up 'til the moment she pushed him out, she swore he was Stanley's son. DNA test results later revealed that "Baby Rag," Lance Jones, was indeed her child's father. Soon after Karisha was released from the hospital and sent back to the women's facility, Baby Rag got full custody of the child, along with a restraining order against Karisha, and he is in the process of changing the child's last name from Stanley's to his own, Jones. It would be years before Karisha could even object to the restraining order, as she has to serve her seven-year sentence for what she did to Lala. It's said that Karisha is now a lesbian, and the girlfriend of one of the most popular inmates in the jail, "Chuck."

After showing up to the block party that day, Averie wasn't able to get out the car. She saw how life was finally going back to normal for everyone around there, and it made her think about herself. She'd lost so much, but it made her appreciate everything that she still had. She drove away from the block that day and never looked back. Making a vow to herself that she would never go back to Compton for as long as she lived, Averie moved to Texas with her best friend. Life is finally looking normal for her again. She comes back to Cali every summer to visit Tony's grave on his birthday, and she often leaves flowers for Stanley as well.

Baby Rag realized that he will always be from the hood, but since the day he laid eyes on his seed and obtained full custody, he knew he could no longer be *for* the hood. Lesson gave him so many reasons to get himself straight. Using the money he had saved over the years, he moved himself, his girlfriend, Raquel, and Lesson to a house he had built in Moreno Valley. The three of them are doing well, and Baby Rag even put his gangbanging days to rest.

Xavier and Lala are set to get married in June 2015. Kamille will be turning one-year-old in a few months, and she is as happy and healthy as can be. Xavier's older daughter, Tia, now lives with Lala and Xavier full-time. Nobody saw their relationship coming, but the two of them shared something that not too many people were good at. They shared a love that nobody saw coming, a love that couldn't compare to anything else in the world. They shared loyalty to one another, even though they started off wrong in society's eyes. It was right in the eyes of those who knew what real love and loyalty looked like.

Love who you want, love who loves you. Don't lie to those you love. *Lies* bring *karma*, and karma doesn't discriminate.

The End

Contact Kiera Thomas online:
Email: kieratanaethomas@gmail.com
Twitter: @authorkaytee
Facebook: https://www.facebook.com/LoveChocDrop

CPSIA information can be obtained at www.ICGtesting.com
Printed in the USA
LVOW12s1536210515

439401LV00010B/881/P